The
Auraless

by Katarina Boudreaux

A THURSTON HOWL PUBLICATIONS BOOK

ISBN 978-1-945247-20-0

The Auraless

Edited by Sherayah Witcher

A Thurston Howl Publications Book
Published by Thurston Howl Publications
thurstonhowlpublications.com
Knoxville, TN

Cover design by Tabsley

Printed in the United States of America
10 9 8 7 6 5 4 3 2 1

Dedication: For Kuillin, dreams, and imagination. To my family, thank you for the endless support and love—I'm a lucky one.

THE SPEAKING

DIFFERENT SHAPES FLASH across the screen. I focus on the ones that are most attractive to me. I Feel their power. I blink my eyes three times when the screen returns to white—the combination of all colors.

Nothing happens. Which is good.

The testing apparatus—a semi-circular metal device that fits around my head—is too tight over my ears. I reposition it while it quantifies my choices. A warning bell rings.

I stop moving the apparatus and focus on the screen. Plain text rolls across the screen. I skim it. I have read the information many times. I stretch my arms and wish that my sleeves were looser like the younger held's clothing. My pants are wide and comfortable, as is fitting my age.

The next challenge pops up on the view screen. I focus on the shapes and changing colors. Only two shapes are consistently colored in primary shades. I blink my eyes definitively three times.

The screen changes quickly to a series of lines, some of which are partially colored. I repeat the blinking process.

The constant blinking makes me dizzy. I close my eyes and hope that I answered the challenges quickly enough so that I do not have to read the next history. The testing apparatus buzzes, so I am compelled to read.

Auras became more apparent when the great time of Coloration began for the Indigo Children.

I try to imagine what the original Auraed Paix looked like. Their auras were uncontrolled and visible. Now, they look human, with the posterior chamber of the eye colored according to Aura type.

The screen shifts. The next segment of text is about which color developed first on the Aura wheel. The order is important, as Paix is organized into radiating color sections. Red developed first, with all its dynamic creativeness. Blue came after, then orange and green.

"For some," I think.

The warning bell rings, so I sit straighter in the testing chair. It is tempting to speak my answers, but I am testing and cannot. I am given a test on what I have read. I choose answers by blinking and wait.

The next screen comes quickly. I study the view screen closely. Several colors are represented in the corners. Empty space is in the center of the screen. I focus on the corners without hesitation, then blink and re-focus on the center of the screen. I wait. The screen changes to text about the continued rise of the Auraed.

"For some."

I think about how those without Auras must have felt—jealous, scared. Colorless. The new Auraed children could connect to each other in a fully collective manner. Information, not just Words, could be passed between them via thought. They already knew what their parental units knew at birth. And with their collective intelligence, they were vastly more intelligent than a single unit.

Exactly like now. The Auraed have intelligence that the Auraless will never have.

The next screen materializes. Different colors are woven across it. I choose the dark space on the periphery, then blink my eyes three times.

"Focus."

The screen goes static before the segment on Paix lineage begins. The lines are detailed back to the Indigo Children and end with our shared ancestry. I find my parents' names under their color and spance, and then my own name.

"Pass."

The Auraless are the Paix's new history. I repeat the Paix label for me in my mind: "Lisle, Subject 46." I was born without an Aura. There are only 156 Auraless like me. We were all born within the last twenty spances. Some spances, there were more Auraless delivered, some spances less. Six spances ago, there were no Auraless born.

"Think."

There must be a reason for our abnormality. I want to discover it. I am very close to passing the test and connecting to the Paix . . .

The screen blinks, and the text disappears. I tense, fully attentive. The next screen is my stumbling block. I have never been able to pass it. The screen is blank. I must connect to understand what information the mix of colors holds. I study it.

The testing apparatus buzzes. My time to choose is running out. I close my eyes and Drift. I open my eyes, focus aimlessly, then blink three times.

Nothing happens for a moment, and I think that maybe this time, I have passed. The view screen flickers, once, twice . . . then the testing apparatus shuts off.

"Failure. Again."

CHAPTER 1

When the Fusion Wars broke out, Listener drones took over the sky. Originally designed by the Triumphant for use against their enemy, the Republic, the Listener drones decimated the human population of Earth. Sound became deadly.

—HISTORIES OF PAIX, INDIGO 1.1

I AM FLOATING. TENDRILS of thought twist tightly around my wrists and bind me. Disturbed by the sensation, I pull my left arm to my chest. It will not comply. I pull harder. Something nudges me several times in the ribs, and I strike out with my right hand.

"Stop fighting, Lisle. Wake. It is Jaigon."

Jaigon is leaning over me. He smells like the forest that surrounds our Koja. There are lines creasing his forehead. I touch his cheek to soothe his worry away until I realize that I am no longer sleeping. I draw my hand back quickly.

My eyes adjust to the dark. My best friend, Mon, is still sleeping. She sleeps on top of her sheets. Our twin roommates Par and Vena are also still asleep. Par's hand trails off her bed and touches the floor. Vena's blanket is wrapped around her body tightly.

I peer up at the glass ceiling. The Earth is dark, and shadows trail down the seven-foot-high white-washed walls that frame our room. The sun has not risen. So no one could have given Jaigon permission to enter. "Who allowed you entry?"

Jaigon pulls the covers away from my body. "I allowed me entry. Come, trust me."

Something is wrong. Jaigon's voice is low and tense. His dark hair is unruly, and I can barely distinguish the whiteness of his eyes from the darkness of his skin. He offers me his hand. I do not take it. I am furious that he has invaded my room. "I am not happy about your presence in my room. But I will comply with your wishes."

"Good enough."

I do not tidy the bed, as I hope to come back to it. My covers are gray and comfortable, and I hate to leave them. My whole room is comfortably plain—straight metal shelving, furniture made of colorless plastic, textureless walls decorated with a six-inch-wide painted line of each different Aura. We share a bathroom with a small mirror, shower, sink, and toilet. The bathroom is not decorated, as it is used only for personal Ablution.

"Hurry, Lisle. Before the rest of the Koja wakes. Keep your sleeping apparel on."

"All right, all right." My sleeping apparel consists of gray shorts and a beige, soft cotton shirt. The Paix provide us with waking and sleeping clothes, so we all dress the same according to age except at meals and Rituals. I put my hair in a ponytail with a slim, rainbow-colored cord and slip on my black, Auraless issued shoes.

I walk out the door behind Jaigon and follow him around our winding Calle. We duck in some spots where the ceiling is low. Pretty plants hang from the ceiling in every corner. They have long leaves and white, dainty flowers. There are blinking lights recessed into the walls. They are programmed by the Paix's Ortus to recognize our motion and blink in a rainbow of colors next to us until we reach the primary Salle.

I skim the wall with my fingertips. This Salle's ceiling is fifteen feet high and also made of glass. It rests on top of six foot, rainbow colored walls. The walls curve and do not form corners. Recessed circles have different colored reflective lights that activate when the Paix are present in our dwelling.

Our Koja is warm and familiar here, like a living being. The Central Lexicon, located where the Salle's and Calle's intersect, is the heart of our Koja. It connects us to the Ortus. The primary Salles and Calles function as arteries, our rooms and other areas, organs.

At this time of the morning, it is quiet. Normally, the sound of voices fills the Salles and Calles as the Auraless move to work, school, or play. It is so quiet, I hear my feet patter on the smooth, clear floor. I see the soil of the Earth beneath me through it.

It is also emotionally quiet. I Feel nothing. It is a freeing sensation, and I enjoy the moment. With just Jaigon, I can ignore the emotional eddies. It is more difficult in groups to not Feel.

We exit the Koja closest to the cliffs. It is my favorite entrance/exit, as the clear glass has silver and gold metal beams patterned like arching rainbows as supports. Drops of color drip from each rainbow in perfect circles.

The forest welcomes us, even at this hour. I hear bird calls, and purple and white flowers bloom from hanging vines near our pathway. Squirrels scamper across our path, and I see the tail of a chipmunk before it dives into a golden-leafed bush. The trees are tall and sway gently. Needles line the path like a blanket for our feet.

I take a better look at Jaigon. His shirt is darker than mine, as is customary for his age, but it is torn in two places. It is unlike Jaigon to be unkempt. His eyes are haggard and his hair uncombed. "Have you rested?"

Jaigon shakes his head no. He takes my hand and holds it tightly. "All will be explained."

I Feel Jaigon needs to hold my hand, so I let him, though it makes me uncomfortable. Once, there were no secrets between us, but now there is an awkward distance. I try to Drift, but my Being resists being open, perhaps because of the early hour. I have never tried to Drift before the Paix and Auraless time of rising.

"Failure."

I quit trying after several minutes effort and endeavor to keep up with Jaigon's pace.

"Just a little further."

Jaigon and I took walks frequently before my age of reckoning—sixteen. Since then, I feel he has avoided spending Solitary time with me. I do not blame him, as being a Feeler makes people hesitant to spend time with you. There are no surprises.

A hawk swoops from the sky and lands in a nearby tree. I marvel at the ease of its motion and wiggle my fingers. "Why must we walk so fast?"

Jaigon does not respond.

"Focus."

Even though it is early, the temperature is normalized. The Paix's Yuan controls all aspects of our atmosphere and protects us from the Helio. I do not understand the Yuan or how it works, although I know from the Lexicon that it is considered one of the greatest post-Fusion war achievements of the Paix.

I have seen the edge of the Yuan spances ago on an away trip with my history class. It had looked like soft glass. Beyond it is the Far, where everything is flat, blurry, and strangely beige. I had felt lonely observing the Far.

Jaigon Feels like that now—desperate and far away. I stop myself from Feeling more, though it is hard with my Talent. I need Words to keep myself in the moment. "Jaigon, can you explain how the collective's Yuan controls our habitat?"

"It functions."

"Yes, it does." There are twenty-one stones the size of a ten held child arranged in the clearing of the stone circle. The trees are a richer shade of green here. The air is heavier, and I Feel a greater sense of connection within myself.

Jaigon puts his arm around my shoulder. "Look."

Shock registers in my Being as I see what Jaigon wants me to notice. A broken body is within the stone circle. The clothes are stained and torn, but clearly belong to an elder held.

"Did an accident occur? Is not that . . ." Words stick in my throat as I recognize the figure on the ground. A wave of nausea overcomes me, and I double over. The ground spins. I put my hands on my knees.

"Els, Subject 32," Jaigon says grimly. He pats my back. "Take deep breaths. Her clothes were in disarray when I found her. I had to carry her here."

I breathe through my mouth several times. "Carried her?"

Jaigon's face is grim. His eyes are flat and his mouth set in a firm line. "Yes."

"Were you with her?" I Feel guilt in Jaigon's Being. Another wave of nausea hits me as I consider that Jaigon may be involved.

"I could not sleep, so walked by the sea. I found her. It was gruesome. I tried to resuscitate her, but she had already Ceased. I carried her to the cliff top to avoid the tide, but then continued to the circle. It is sacred and more fitting."

I want to tell him that it is not his fault, but as Leadership, I know that he feels responsible for all of us. "Did she trip?"

"No. Look at the swelling. The bones in her head were crushed by blunt force. She has been murdered."

"It cannot be." The idea is inconceivable and frightening at the same time. There has never been a murder in the history of the Paix.

"Yet it is. Look at the wounds."

"I do not need to look. Murder has been eradicated from our society."

"From Paix society," Jaigon says ruefully and rubs his thumb across my cheekbone. "And yet, Els, our sister, is dead."

I like the way Jaigon's finger Feels on my face.

"Focus on the present."

"There has been no murder in the histories for the last

thousand years. It is against our kind's laws, too."

Jaigon shows me Els's hands. Ugly gashes are cut evenly across both wrists. Splotches of blood stain the ground beneath her. "To accomplish one slice at this angle, without assistance, is possible. Two, it is not."

I finally accept Jaigon's Words. "Who would do such a thing? It is . . . violent."

"There are only two options," Jaigon responds. "The Paix, or one of us. The Indentured cannot deviate from their programming. Can you Drift? It is important to know if it was a Paix."

"My Talent is not like that. I do not command it. I open myself to the collective around us, and sometimes it happens. I Drift. But I am only on the periphery. Never inside."

"You reported that you are closer to understanding the connection."

I look at Els. Her face is contorted. She does not look peaceful. "Yes. It is like a weight that you carry around with you all the time that is yours, but not connected to you."

Jaigon stares into my eyes, and I notice how beautifully brown and Auraless his eyes are. They seem almost black in the thin, early morning light. "I . . ."

Jaigon cuts me off. "Try later. I need to know the general temperament of the collective mind after this is reported. I know you can accomplish that much. You have this image to connect with. We must return to the Koja."

"What are you going to do?"

"Notify the Nagid. Call the Assembly and pow wow."

"It is the logical course of action, as written in the Paix's laws. I wonder if Els's Paix family . . ."

Jaigon does not let me complete my Words. "Do not wonder. Focus on Drifting. That is your duty to our Koja."

An uneasiness takes root in my Being. I do not know if I can fulfill my duty adequately. We return to the Koja in silence, and Jaigon directs me to report to my quarters and await the Summons and renewal of the day.

The Salle is still eerily quiet. I raise my hand in greeting when I encounter Druce and Saul, who are in charge of preparing the meal this morn. They are surprised by my presence, and I Feel their curiosity. When I come to Els's quarters, I mark my passing with the Paix symbol of farewell—four fingers together with the thumb bent across the palm.

I touch the access pad, and the door to my room slides open. Mon is awake and raises her eyebrows, but does not ask questions. Par and Vena are still asleep.

I cross the room to the bathroom, and the door secures behind me. The image of Els encircled by the stones haunts me, and I have to physically rid myself of the smell and feel of the experience. I peel my clothes off and place them in the Replicator. I am glad I will never wear them again. I step into the Ablution receptacle, which is a six-foot, clear tube. The water is activated when I line my feet up on the rainbow-colored pad on the floor. A soap dispenser slides out from the wall, and I complete my Ablution.

The water shuts off, and I step out of the receptacle. A metallic grate on the floor opens, and I step in. A strong, hot blast of air encompasses me. After three minutes, I step out. The grate slides shut. I am clean, but still see Els's lifeless body in my mind's eye.

"Focus."

I open the Replicator's basket and take out the fresh clothes prepared for me. I put them on and turn to the sink. I wave my hand over a finger-sized, white box, and a white pill appears in a vertical pull-out tray. I take it, put it in my mouth, and swish it around. Teeth cleaned, I exit the bathroom and return to my bed. Mon signs to me a question mark, but I pull the covers over my head and wait.

The Summons from Jaigon comes twenty minutes later via our personal Lexicons. The day's renewal alarm sounds immediately after. The sharp chirp wakes Par and Vena. They chatter about their classes for the day and compare dreams. I tidy my sheets and wait for Mon to complete Ablutions. When she is ready, we tell Par and Vena goodbye and exit. The lights on the wall light up and follow behind us like lit shadows.

Mon looks at me inquisitively. "I wonder what Assembly is all about. I bet someone knows."

"We will all know in a short time."

The lights stop near the end of the second hallway. We are not near the Salon. I move forward, then back. The lights do not follow my motion. "The lights are malfunctioning."

"Report it to Mechanical," Mon says. "Better yet, I can go and tell them. I rather like the Mechanicals."

I giggle, as Mon is always hanging around the Mechanical wing. She says she is just curious, but I Feel there is more to it than that. "Any particular Mechanical?"

"Any will do. They know how things work."

"Ah." I walk with my hand raised with fingers extended upwards in Greeting to all the other Auraless gathering with us.

Our first task of the day is to break the fast. We file into the Dispensary. The ceiling is made of triangular-twisted metal in the rainbow pattern. The walls are transparent. Seven low, white tables are set up across the room—four parallel and three perpendicular. The legs of each table are one solid Paix wheel color. There are no chairs, but individual cushions are recessed into the floor and match the nearest leg color.

"Greetings," I say to the Replicator and scan my hand. A series of three dots line up on the screen, and I retrieve my meal. It is wrapped in Indigo paper.

Mon moans. "I hate Indigo day."

Since there are seven colors on the Paix color wheel, each day we receive a different supplemental and meal plan consistent with Paix color. Indigo is a corn-and-blueberry-based round cake. Mon dislikes blueberries. I do not mind them, but prefer orange day. Violet is my least favorite day.

The Dispensary is filled with conversation, particularly about the Assembly that has been called. I Feel the emotion runs the gamut from worry to ambivalence. Elias, a particularly precocious middle held, puts his whole cake in his mouth and pretends to be Paix. He walks around with his hands outstretched and his eyes closed.

"Elias," Marisol scolds. "Sit down and consume your food."

Elias sits but does not take the cake from his mouth. Marisol takes it from him. All older helds serve a turn at Dispensary as monitor to make sure the younger and middle helds behave and eat properly. I Feel high emotions radiating from the middle helds and am sorry for Marisol.

"Elias will be Leadership one day," Mon comments and finishes her cake. "The others of his age follow his example."

"I can only hope he grows out of this stage."

Feinz, our classmate, leans over my shoulder. "What is Assembly about, Lisle?"

Feinz does not complete his Ablutions on schedule, and I wrinkle my nose. "I do not know. I Feel. I am not a mind reader."

Mon winks at me. "Perhaps a discourse on personal hygiene?"

Feinz is oblivious to Mon's intent. "What do you Feel?"

I Feel that Feinz is nervous, which means he did not do something he was supposed to. That is his personality, forgetful and unreliable. "I Feel that you have forgotten something."

Feinz's eyebrows shoot up, and he hurries away.

Mon laughs. "Did you really Feel that?"

"An educated guess. Poor Feinz."

A loud bell strikes the hour, followed by a smaller gong. It is time for the older helds to study Paix history and have personal growth time, and for the younger helds to study mathematics and language arts. They are read a Paix history lesson before their evening sleep. It is simplified for their enjoyment.

Mon wipes our table clean. "I am tired. I think I will nap through Paix class."

"You cannot. The Lexicon will alert you of your lack of attention."

"I have been thinking up a plan to fool the Lexicon."

"History is not that bad," I say encouragingly. "We are almost to the end of the Fusion Wars."

"It never ends," Mon says. "How old is the Paix, after all?"

"We do not know definitively. They are Ancient."

We walk arm in arm to our classroom. It is the largest of the Paix history classrooms and shaped like a crescent. Our learning modules are tilted circles with individual screens adjusted for our heights. My module is three away from Mon at the end of the row.

Mon salutes me. "See you after part three of the war. Only fifteen million to go."

I giggle and leave Mon at her module. I enter mine and settle into the seat. It molds to my form, and I relax. I have always enjoyed history, and I look forward to the lesson.

Gertrude, who is assigned the module on my left, sticks her head into my module. "Who do you think wins?"

"The Paix, in the end."

"Right, you are," Gertrude says and sighs. "Too bad we have to watch it."

"You can always practice your . . ."

Gertrude steps into her module. I Feel that she is frustrated, and I understand why. Two hours of Paix history followed by a pass or fail test is stressful, and Gertrude struggles. Her Talent is Mechanical.

The lights dim, and I wait for my screen to light up. I pay attention as the screen begins to move. It changes shape to accentuate the information presented. The first hour is spent in image recognition with rudimentary words describing the screen. The second hour is spent in reading the Paix history as recorded by the Indigo.

The time for the test arrives, and I am ready. The screen buzzes, and I engage the answer pad with my right hand. It is smooth and round and seven-sided. The screen fizzles, and a series of rainbow-colored lines appear.

"Error," I say clearly.

The screen does not change.

I Feel indecision in the room. I peek out the side of the

module. Gertrude is standing outside her module. Several other Auraless are wandering around the room. The lights are on.

Mon steps into my module and sits next to me. "The room has flipped to Cleaning mode."

"But it is not the proper time. Not for hours."

Mon pats the side of my module. "Nevertheless, Cleaning is taking place. You know, I think your module is more comfortable than mine."

"It is the same."

Mon pushes me out of my module. "Go see what is happening. I am going to get that nap after all."

"Do not complain when you have to repeat the class." Mon closes her eyes and feigns sleep. "Fine. I will investigate."

I walk to the window. A thin stream of water is trickling down the outside of the wall. Large wiper blades move from the ceiling to the floor. Four Indentured males manually move the wiper blades back to the top of the ceiling.

Paix history explains how the Indentured came to live with the Paix. The Indentured are damaged Paix that mixed with the pre-Ancients. Their progeny continues to flourish. The Paix care for them by correcting their genetic deformities and giving them programming to help them lead productive lives. In return, the Indentured work for the Paix.

I touch the glass. "It is not the right time. Abort."

One of the Indentured males looks at me. His eyes do not focus on mine. His neck is partially metal, and he directs the other three Indentured with a bionic arm. He is dressed in robes that do not fit him, and he does not wear shoes. I have had little contact with the Indentured, as they do not speak and are programmed by the Paix.

"It is not the proper hour for Cleaning," I say.

The Indentured male moves the wiper blade back to the top of the glass.

"Perhaps their programming has malfunctioned," Gertrude says.

I step away from the wall. Of course, that is why they are cleaning at an incorrect time. I sigh. Sometimes, I can be dramatic. "Yes. You are right."

The Auraless of my age convene in different groups and chatter. I do not Feel tension, but relief. I return to my module and stand next to it. I do not wait long, as a long gong sounds before I am tired of standing.

"Mon," I say and tap my module. "Wake up."

"I am awake."

"The Tending gong . . ."

"Yes, I heard it."

I pause. Mon does not exit the module. "Mon . . ."

"Oh, all right," Mon says. "Let us tend, even though it is early."

The rest of the class partner with their workmate before walking out of the glass sliding doors at the far end of the classroom. We no longer need to produce our own food, as the Replicators provide for our needs, but it is our custom to work the fields as our ancestors did to produce our nooning meal. We wind up the path through a manicured field. Several Indentured are working. They are at their appointed, correct tasks. I raise my hand in Greeting. None of them respond.

Mon raises her eyebrows. "You know they are programmed?"

"As well as you do," I reply. "But I Feel something from them. Guarded emotion. Confusion. The Cleaning, the Assembly . . . even they know that something is not right."

"The Paix is off today," Mon says. "I never thought I would say that."

I do not want to admit that the Paix is acting abnormal. It makes me worry. I think about Els. "It may be a new schedule relating to Assembly. We do not understand their ways."

Mon shakes her head. We continue down the path and come to a gravel embankment, then to the terra farming area that the Paix has allotted to us. The earth is divided into seven ascending levels. Different crops are planted on each level according to color. It looks like a giant, multi-colored flower opening to the sky.

"What do you want to harvest today?"

"Herbs," I say. "I would like to add them to our Shab meal."

"For the nooning meal, silly. Herbs are welcome any time of day."

We climb the Indigo stairs and make our way to the plot designated for our needs. Par and Vena are already harvesting. "Gourds? Did you tend your green beds?"

"Yes, yes. We have greens."

I raise my hand in Greetings to Par and Vena. They reciprocate. "Then that is our nooning meal."

"Better than Indigo fare."

I am not sure I agree with Mon, as I prefer replicated food. I kneel in front of the gourd bed and turn the dirt over with my fingers. The soil feels chalky and thin. "This has not been watered."

"Course, it has," Par says. "Did you aerate efficiently?"

"Yesterday," I reply. I touch the leaves of the gourds. They are brittle. "And yes. These must be harvested today, Mon. The plant is dying. Help me."

Mon kneels beside me. "They were fine yesterday."

I twist the gourds from their stems. "I will report it. Perhaps the irrigation system needs maintenance."

Mon and I work to save the gourds we have cared for. There are twelve on the row of plants, more than enough for our nooning meal.

"Par, Vena," Mon calls. "Do not harvest. Share our meal."

Par takes three of the gourds from our pile. "Thank you."

Par and Vena walk down the steps to the Replicators lined up against the embankment. We still have too many gourds. "What shall we do with the rest?"

Mon shrugs her shoulder. "I would rather eat a supplemental pack. Actually, I would really rather know what Assembly is about."

I stand. "We will dry them in the Replicator. I have never had dried gourd, but it cannot be too bad."

Mon makes a choking noise. "Dried gourd. Sounds appetizing."

I wipe the dirt from my hands on my pants and look around the third tier. An Indentured female is repairing a water tube. Her circular metal hat glistens in the sunlight. My hair moves across my face, and I shudder. "Was that . . . a breeze?"

Mon looks up at me. "I felt nothing."

I touch my forehead and look at my hand.

"What would a breeze be doing this time of day? That is only used at night to cleanse the air."

The Indentured female sits on the terrace. Her face is slack, and she folds her hands across her chest as if she is dead.

"Failure."

"Yes, I know. The Indentured female . . ."

"Is resting." Mon puts her arm in mine. "Probably part of her programming. Work, rest. And now for us—dried gourds. A feast of gourds. Let us go."

I let Mon lead me down the terrace, but I look back at the Indentured female. She has not moved. Mon loads the Replicator with our overharvest and receives two plates of cooked gourd and several cloth bags of dried gourd. The bags are held shut with rainbow colored ribbon.

"I foresee midnight snacks."

The Indentured female stands and returns to her task. I sigh in relief.

"Lisle?"

Mon snaps her finger in front of my face. "Are you Drifting?"

"No, the Indentured . . ."

Mon shoves a plate into my hands. "Leave the Indentured alone. Eat. Assembly is up next. Care to shed some light on it?"

I shake my head no and eat my plate of food. It tastes bland and chalky.

CHAPTER 2

The drones determined the vocal pitch frequency of enemy human-oids. After the Listener's internal Lexicon homed in on the singular pitch, it eliminated the identified Being by poison gas.

—HISTORIES OF PAIX, INDIGO 1.1.5

WE REACH THE SALON's sliding doors. Half of the Auraless have already entered the Salon. Faint arches decorate the outside, clear brick walls.

Mon hisses, "What is he doing here? He reminds me more of a blue dragon every time I see him. His teeth and talons get sharper as he ages."

Ditero is standing in the center of the Salon with Jaigon. He is a descendant of the original Indigo family and our representative from the Nagid—the Paix council that cares for our needs. His eyes are rimmed with Indigo, and he is dressed in a prim Indigo suit. His woven, colored shoes that those with Auras are given at birth look even brighter than normal to me.

"Dragons did not exist," I say stiffly. "They were of imagination. And Indigo is not blue."

"So serious. I wonder if he has been wearing those shoes since birth."

"You know they cannot be worn until the age of reckoning."

"Maybe he was born sixteen spances," Mon says and grins evilly. "I know things. Born old, trust me."

I join the line to enter the Salon. The ceiling is a pointed glass dome with geometrical triangles framing the sky. Circular chairs made of primary Paix colors are arranged in curved rows. I enter the Salon and wait next to the rectangular, waist-high Lexicon. I hold up my hand. The Lexicon's computerized eye recognizes my palm print, then records my attendance.

"Subject 46," I say clearly. The light on top of its surface turns … green. I walk through and wait for Mon.

"Is the Lexicon lagging?" Mon asks. "It is green today and yesterday. It should be Indigo. Bad food equals Indigo. Or did I miss something?"

The color is off, as each day of the week is a different color with no repetition. "It should be Indigo today."

It takes another five minutes for all of the Auraless to convene. Everyone whispers out of respect for Ditero's position and status. Jaigon raises his hand when the Salon is full, and we cease speaking Words.

Mon and I sit near the center of the Salon with others of our age. She nudges me and makes motions with her hands as if she is playing the flute. "Stop," I whisper.

I Feel Ditero watching me. Tendrils of collective thought pour from him. They are heavy and confused. Different. I wish I could see them in color.

"Are you listening to him? You have that look on your face again."

I shake my head no, but Ditero continues to look in my direction. I hold his gaze for a moment and think I hear voices, but they are murky at best.

Failure. Departure. Failure. Departure. Failure. Departure.

I shake my head and cover my ears with my hands. The voice is clear and powerful, oppressive with an echo. Other voices are like a roar behind it. The noise in my head becomes deafening. I am losing my mind. Ditero raises his hand suddenly, and the voice stops.

"He thinks you are listening to him," Mon whispers.

"I am not. I cannot listen, as I cannot connect. Now stop," I mutter. My mind is chaotic and slow. This experience is unlike any I have had, and it terrifies me. I look at my hands and clench them. I focus on my own thoughts.

"Lisle. My name is Lisle."

Ditero turns back to Jaigon. He takes out his communication device. The Lexicon above the entrance finally turns Indigo.

Ditero relaxes, and so do I. I watch him interact with the Lexicon by moving his eyes. I don't mind him most of the time. He is more comfortable around the Auraless than most of the other Paix because of his studies. But the new voice . . .

"His eyes are really intense," Mon whispers.

I nod in agreement. Ditero's every movement is intense. "Maybe studying our Words makes him more austere."

Mon sniffs. "Not likely."

I think it is more likely than Mon believes. Even though the Paix has evolved past letters for communication, the direct descendants of the original Indigo Children make the study of written Word their life's work. They developed a translator to communicate with us, so that our Words create pictures for them. "Indigo minds are suited for the intense individual focus necessary for reading. They function best in Singular. Without them . . ."

Mon cuts me off with a wave of her hand. "Yes, yes. We would never be able to understand each other."

"If we even do fully now."

A loud buzz fills the Salon. I Feel the emotions of the Auraless shift from curiosity to apprehension. I focus on Ditero and Jaigon.

"Thank you for your presence," Jaigon begins. "I have called this Assembly for discussion. We are the Auraless, and our representative from the Paix is in attendance. Ditero 532 of Indigo descent."

We all know Ditero, but the introduction is part of the Paix Ritual and must be spoken. Ditero looks around the room slowly. He bows his head.

Jaigon indicates the room with his right hand, then brings his hand to his heart. "I speak for the Auraless."

"Present," we all say in unison. I Feel a range of emotions, but mostly anxiety and curiosity, horror. Every Auraless knows that Assembly is only called if something serious has occurred.

"One of us has Ceased," Jaigon says in a calm voice. "Our sister Els, Subject 32."

Several Auraless gasp and murmur. I Feel confusion and disbelief in the Auraless. Mon squeezes my hand. "That, you could have told me."

I shake my head no and mouth the Word, "Later."

"I ask for information," Jaigon says in a louder voice and brings both his arms up to shoulder height. He opens his arms towards us, then drops them slowly to his sides according to Paix Ritual. "I open the floor for Illumination."

No one rises to speak.

After several seconds of silence, Ditero hands Jaigon the Lexicon translator. It is Indigo with a rainbow casing, and the screen is multi-dimensional for the Auraless' benefit. Jaigon picks through pictures. I use a similar device when communicating short phrases to my parents. The patience required to explain hard concepts or long stories is beyond my Being.

"Focus on the present."

I Feel Jaigon's relief when he finally completes inputting data into the Lexicon. He hands the translator back to Ditero.

The exchange of concepts is always slow. Ditero takes his time deciphering the information, then responds to Jaigon's pictorial explanation in the same fashion. When he is done, he hands the

Lexicon back to Jaigon and clicks his heels ceremoniously.

Jaigon reads, and I scoot forward on the edge of my seat. Ditero closes his eyes. Time seems to slow in the Salon.

Finally, Jaigon stamps his right foot and nods. This is the Paix gesture to indicate acceptance. Ditero displays the image holographically for all to see. Jaigon opens his arms and reads the Words aloud. "Ditero has contacted the collective Paix for information. There is little record of Els. Her parents have not seen her in over ten spances, as visitation was determined to be unnecessary for both parties. The collective mind holds no recent recognition of her whereabouts."

It is common that the Auraless stop seeing their parents at some point, but I am surprised that the collective consciousness has no recent recollection of Els, as her palm was scanned regularly by the Lexicon in her daily routine. "That's impossible," I whisper to Mon. She pantomimes sleeping.

"Further investigation will be handled by the Auraless," Jaigon continues. He takes the Lexicon from Ditero and begins the process of choosing pictures and words from the Lexicon again. He returns the Lexicon to Ditero.

Ditero types into the Lexicon, then displays it holographically for us all to read.

A murmur of surprise fills the Salon. The Paix Ritual requires that Leadership, in this case Jaigon, read the decision before it is presented to the Auraless.

We all read the words. "Murder is not allowed in Paix."

I Feel the room's emotional atmosphere fill with panic and fear.

"It is not allowed," Jaigon states. He does not type into the Lexicon, as the Ritual was broken by Ditero.

Ditero closes his eyes. He opens them after several seconds. I can see how Indigo the rims truly are. His implant is barely noticeable. He does not say words of Parting, but instead exits the Salon.

My jaw drops. "There was no Parting offered or received."

"Murder may not be on the Ritual plate," Mon says. "It looks bad."

I think about murder, then of Els. I try to remember the sound of her voice. We were never close, but I cannot get the image of the blankness of her dead eyes out of my mind. I shiver, and Mon pinches my arm.

"That hurts," I say in surprise.

"Tell me things next time."

Jaigon sweeps the Salon with his gaze. He looks at the ground and clenches his fists. His Words are clipped, and I Feel his unhappiness. "We will attend to the Finalities now. Class will be held immediately following. We meet this evening for continued discourse on this matter."

"No one spoke aloud when he opened the floor," I hear whispered from someone behind me. I Feel panic escalate in the Auraless.

"We should support Jaigon," I say to Mon. "He seems fragile. Many are upset."

"Fragile?" Mon chokes out.

I give Mon a hard look. "It is a lot of pressure being the Leadership. He is responsible for EVERYTHING here."

"He can handle himself."

Several Auraless are already standing. Mon and I join our assigned lines. We file out of the Salon according to group and spance. I am unable to focus on my own feelings, as I cannot stop the feelings of the Auraless from filtering into my consciousness.

The intrusive feelings lessen when we exit the Koja. The air is fragrant and calming, the trees familiar and pleasant. Our group is silent as we walk. The new Auraless have never attended Finalities before, though they are part of our school curriculum.

This is my second Finalities. Subject 7 had died early of an unknown disease. The Paix had sent representatives, but the parents of Subject 7 had not attended. Subject 7 had never connected to his parents mentally, so they did not Feel the loss as we did.

The edge of the sea is only forty yards from our Koja, and we line up in numerical order with every ten Beings making a new line. I am in the second line. I am glad, as it gives me separation.

The hair pricks on the back of my neck. Someone is watching me. I look to the East. An Indentured female is standing near the edge of the cliff. Her eyes lock with mine. She is crying. I raise my hand in greeting, but the Indentured female turns and shuffles away.

The trees do not seem as green now. Everything connected to the Paix must Feel the loss of Els. Even the Indentured. And yet no one from the Paix is in attendance to supervise. I am surprised, as normally, they are very zealous in the punctual performance of the Rituals and Rites. It preserves their tie to us.

"It feels empty," the girl next to me says. "There is no Paix."

I nod in agreement. Her name is Shenandoah, and she radiates sadness. I wish I did not Feel it. I pat her arm. "We are here."

"Els was really nice," Shenandoah says and looks away from me.

"Yes. Let us respect this time."

Jaigon raises the Ritual Lexicon to begin the ceremony. This Lexicon's color is Red, as is suiting for Finalities. Red is the Paix color of life and death.

Our oldest held, Sarta, Subject 1, stands next to Jaigon. She is wearing a rainbow-colored robe that shimmers in the light. Her clothing is closest to that of the Paix as she is the first of our kind. She did not want to have Leadership, so she transferred her right to Jaigon. She still participates in Ritual as Leadership.

Some of the younger children are squirming. I flash the Paix Prohibere sign—a triangle made with both hands. Since our group is Feelers, many are in my movement class, and they look at the ground instead of right at me.

"Respect, younger helds," I say firmly. Mon begins to play her flute, and I center myself to participate in the Ritual. The melody is constructed to lift our spirits in prayer to the sky and the wind.

"We gather for the Finalities of Els, Subject 32. Auraless. Born of Strand 13, Tether 19, Paix," Jaigon says in a clear, ringing voice.

The entirety of the Auraless repeat Jaigon's words. I repeat them as well, but think about what the numbers really represent—Auraless birth number, Paix address. The Paix live in Tethers and Strands organized by Aura color and family.

"Subject 32 will be Recorded in the Tome of the Auraless," Jaigon says loudly. One of the older helds, Chur, stands and lifts the Lexicon of the Auraless. It does not have a color.

We repeat his words, then turn as one unit to the East. Four masked Auraless walk along the shore of the sea. Their masks represent the Aura wheel, with Red being the predominant Ritual color. Els's body is carried between them on a flat piece of etched glass. The etchings are of arches and stars, with the color wheel circumscribed in the middle. She is completely wrapped in red cloth with silver circles sewn in an overlapping pattern across the edges. The shoes of her Paix birthright are placed on either side of her body. Since she is Auraless, they cannot be put on her feet.

I stare at her bare feet. Even in death, she cannot claim her birthright.

"Do not let your Talent control your Being."

"The body rests," Jaigon declares as the four masked Auraless place the body on the ground at his feet. "Our thoughts shall rest with it."

Sarta raises her hands to shoulder height and walks over Els from her head to her feet two times. "As the first, I rename thee Sky and bid you safe travels."

Sarta lowers her arms and looks at the gathering. We answer with shrieks that approximate what wind would sound like whipping across a jagged mountain top.

The four masked Auraless pick up Els's body and walk in a Westerly direction away from us. They will leave Els's body on the second tier of the abandoned cliffs five kilometers away. When the birds and elements take pieces of her, she will return to the sky and the wind from whence we all came.

This is the way of the Auraless alone. The Paix return to the Ortus—the beginning and end of all Paix life. Even in the womb, the Paix child is connected to the Ortus via its mother's implant. The departed Paix's shell and implant are returned to the Ortus for recycling.

The Ritual is complete, and the lines disperse. I Feel the sadness of the Auraless around me. It weighs me down. My class begins in twenty minutes, so I start down the well-used cliff path so that I can walk by the sea on my return to the Koja. The sea helps me cope with the burden of emotion I Feel.

I hear a few notes on a flute and look up. Mon is on the cliff top. She waves at me and points in the direction of the Koja. I point to the sea and Mon turns away.

I need time to process. And I am afraid to accept what happened in Assembly.

"You Felt a mind not your own."

"It is dangerous to linger," Jaigon says from behind me.

I jump. I did not hear him approach. His face is like the cliff rock, hard and weathered, even though he is only nineteen spance. I do not wish to argue with him and definitely do not want to share the new connection experience until I understand it more fully. "It has never been dangerous before."

Jaigon blocks my path to the Koja with his body. I realize how much bigger he is than I am, but I do not shrink away. If anything, I try to stand taller.

"You are grieving? If you are to connect to the Paix, you must control these emotions. They do not have them."

I hate when Jaigon counsels me like I am a younger held. "Neither do I," I say angrily and dart around Jaigon. I run toward the Koja. It looks like a beautiful glass bubble rising from the land.

"You cannot control the process. You cannot control the process."

I repeat the sentence several more times in my mind. The weight of my Talent is heavier than the expectations of Jaigon. Or myself.

Jaigon does not follow me, and I am glad that he does not.

CHAPTER 3

The drones were hacked by the Republic and re-hacked by the Triumphant. There were many casualties on both sides, but the Triumphant prevailed due to their greater technological expertise. Those loyal to the Republic eventually fell into silence, outcasts from civilization.

—HISTORIES OF PAIX, INDIGO 1.2

B Y THE TIME I REACH the Koja, I am almost calm. I stop running, breathe, and organize my thoughts. The lights flicker as I enter the Koja—another Lexicon lag. The grand Salle is empty, so I hurry down a secondary Salle to my classroom. The wall lights follow me part of the way, then sputter out.

Failure. Departure.

"I am Lisle. What do you want?"

There is no answer. Several of my students are waiting near the door, so I smile. "Proceed inward," I say brightly and wait for them to enter our room.

Typical Koja classrooms are glass framed with several cube chairs set in rows for ease of learning. Since my class requires space, there are only three chairs next to the glass wall. The rest of the room is bare. I pull several red square mats from an alcove and place them strategically over the see-through plexiglass floor.

"We will wait for the others. But in the meantime, please be creative and warm up." Several of the students move to the center of the floor and stretch. I nod in encouragement.

Movement class is not for all of the Auraless. My students exhibit proficiency in the area of dance or need to explore their bodily movements to excel in their Talent.

"What is this called?" Shahnei asks. She moves her legs in a scissor-like fashion.

I do not know the Paix names for many things I teach, as this knowledge is lost to us. I have learned all I can by watching my Mother and other dancers at Paix gatherings I have attended. I also learn from the old films stored in our Lexicons. "Whatever it may be called in Paix, it is wonderful. Perhaps we can determine an Auraless name for it. Continue to develop it."

My last three students enter class. They are middle helds and very fond of each other. They remind me of Par, Vena, and Mon. They laugh at the same time, and it lifts my spirits.

I open my arms. "Welcome. We are Auraless."

"Present," my students reply.

"Today, our class is about freedom of expression." I Feel the younger helds are unsettled, and I hope an unstructured class will help them process the Finalities.

I begin by playing music stored in the Lexicon. The names of some of the pieces are known to me. "We must feel the music and let our Beings respond to it without the idea of right or wrong. I challenge you to forget speech for a moment and flow as the Paix do."

The students form lines behind me. I close my eyes. "This is Firebird. Feel the movement."

"It sounds old," Aeva says.

Aeva is one of my most promising students, and I welcome her commentary. Her hair is braided in two thick, black plaits and pinned on top of her head. "It is old. From the Ancients before us. Now, close your eyes. Move."

My arms react first, and my feet combine with them automatically. My body sways as if it is not connected to anything but the whim of my imagination. Energy runs along my spine, and life beats within me. I Feel the weight of thousands of years build within my Being. Time ceases. Sound recedes. Heaviness overcomes me, and I fall into darkness, nothingness . . .

What is this? Where am I?

"Lisle."

I hear my name. The silence breaks, and I open my eyes. The music is no longer playing. My students are all looking at me strangely. I focus on Beazle, the ten held boy who called my name. He has dirty blonde hair and wide eyes.

I put my hand on my forehead and take a deep breath. I am dizzy and tired. "Yes, Beazle?"

"You were shining," Beazle says shyly.

"We all shine when we dance," I say kindly and then invite them to join me once more. "Did you feel the energy? What happened to our music? The Lexicon has been lagging all day today. We must complete the lesson."

"No, you had the shine. Like you had one," Beazle continues. Tamar, a dollfaced twelve held girl, nods with him.

I know that I was connected, but I do not want to share this news. The voice speaking in my mind was not my own but did not Feel like the Paix or the first voice from Assembly. I have no answers. I am afraid of these new voices that have no name.

I clap my hands, and music fills the room. It is not the Firebird. Instead, it is a piece I am not familiar with. My students are waiting for my reply. "I do not have an Aura yet, but thank you, Beazle. What color was I shining?"

Beazle puts his hands in his pockets and looks down. "None. You just had a shine."

In my teaching, I have found that the newest Auraless are more willing to please. They are less bound to their Auraed families, as once they are designated as Auraless in the womb, the Auraed parent ceases attempts to connect. We are their only family.

"We were worried," Shahnei whispers. "You were on the ground when the music was loudest. You were talking about murder. Then the music stopped. We did not tell it to."

I touch Shahnei's face and force a smile. She has a birthmark that looks like a star on her forehead. "Do not worry. My Talent is to Feel. I Feel more than what I wish to, sometimes."

Frightened or not, I need to finish the class. I skip the music forward to a Paix piece. "This is a fine place to start fresh."

"What is it like to connect?" Beazle asks.

I do not know the answer to Beazle's question, but it helps me realize something. I am being connected to by unknown entities. I am not in control of the connection. "I can tell you what it is like to Feel and Drift—but you already know that. Perhaps one day, when you find your own Aura, you can tell me."

I grab Shahnei's hand and spin her. "We connect with each other in our Words and movements. So, let us try again. Maybe something that we can all work on together. The Paix Helio dance. For when we perform for the Koja. Practice delivers a good performance."

The students reform a line. I step in front and do arm motions that I copied from the Lexicon. I continue the lesson by adding the corresponding legwork. After several repetitions, I finally put everything together.

Time passes quickly. Class is almost complete, so I play another piece which I do not know the name of and ask the students to stretch. "Think of your body as fluid motion. Reach for the sky above us and the Earth below us."

"Will Els be taken to the sky?" Beazle asks.

I complete the stretching patterns I have devised for the class. When they are complete, I turn to Beazle. "Els is of sky and wind now. More than that, I do not know."

Beazle looks doubtful. "I wondered if... because ..."

"She is of sky and wind," I repeat with more authority. "Els is at rest now."

Beazle gathers his pack. "I do not Feel any different. Should I Feel different?"

"You do not have to. Remember her in respect. That is all that is required."

Beazle nods in acceptance, and I give him a hug. The classroom bell rings, indicating our time is complete.

"Partings," the students say in a disorganized chorus. They file out of the room in three groups and walk noisily down the hall.

"Partings," I respond. I wish that I could connect directly to Beazle and offer him the hope and love that I have for my fellow kind. Words do not do enough to console. It is our greatest weakness as Auraless that we cannot communicate pure truth as the Paix do.

I tidy my classroom and wave my hand over the Lexicon. It deactivates on the first try. "Perhaps it is just a glitch."

The room grows dark a few seconds later, as is customary when the Lexicon is not in use. I cross my arms over my chest and shiver. I dissect the experience with the strange voices in my mind. I consider the possibility that the Paix truly has connected to me, but dismiss it. I do not have an Aura.

"I am a receptacle."

"Lisle, let's race for Free Unit," Mon says from the doorway. "It will get our minds off of Finalities."

Mon's voice rings in the room, and I almost trip. She giggles and enters my classroom. I offer her one of the chair cubes, which she ignores. "Who else would come by after your class to invite you to race? Humm? Ditero?"

The idea is absurd, and I laugh. "I do like racing."

"But who else?"

"No one else. I like racing with you."

Mon's mouth twitches in disappointment. "Of course, you do." She spins ungracefully in the middle of the room.

"Movement is not your Talent."

She faces me and rolls her body like she is in the sea swimming. "You are accomplished at racing. And dancing."

"I inherited movement skills from my Mother."

"Did you?"

I shrug my shoulders. "She cannot tell me."

Mon sits on the chair. We both laugh at my feeble joke attempt. "Humor is not your Talent. Regardless of what we do or do not inherit, I do not know how you teach the younger helds. It would jumble me."

"You could teach them how to play instruments. You do well with the middle helds. The younger helds would probably enjoy it even more."

Mon bounds out of the chair and hooks her arm in mine. She drags me with her out the door. "Or I could just play them and give up on teaching altogether. It was a disaster when I tried to teach you."

Music had never come to me as it does to Mon. I tried some of the Ancient instruments when I was a younger held, but none of them flowed. One thing about discovering your Talent is that sometimes, it is easier to find what is not your Talent. "You have to teach. You are the only one that can play well."

"Maybe. Henry in middle held is catching on. I may soon have competition."

We walk together in companionable silence down the Salle. Mon verbally greets everyone we pass. When the Salle dead ends, we head away from the Salon. We pass the play area for the younger helds. It is a glass-enclosed diamond with ropes and flat surfaces to climb and hide within. Some of the ropes are hung from the ceiling, and a large nylon net is set up in the farthest corner.

I always loved play time as a younger held. Mon and I would play Contagion with others our age until play time was up. I notice a group of children playing the game now. "Contagion never gets old."

"Always did for me," Mon comments. "You always won."

Being a Feeler had its advantages when I was young—I could always find those who hid from me by tracking emotions. "Not always."

"When you tried, you won," Mon says. "Look at Mercy."

Mercy is taller than anyone in the Koja and only an eleven held. She slouches when she walks, and Mon holds her left hand index finger up when we pass her. She straightens up.

"When did you get to be . . ."

"Oh, stop," Mon says. "We are all responsible for the younger and middle helds."

Mon's quick retort gives me pause. "You have never shown interest in Leadership before."

Mon winks at me and holds both hands up for the Lexicon above the racing field's doors to scan her. She is recognized, and the doors slide open. "I am reforming my opinion of Leadership. It calls me. Do you not hear it?"

Since I know Mon is joking, I do not listen. Instead, I enjoy our surroundings. The racing field is an enclosed glass pentagon at the Northernmost corner of our Koja. The lawn outside of the windows is manicured and perfect. There is no forest, just the edge of our building and a drop off.

I love this area of the Koja. It faces the original cliff dwellings. I walk up to the glass window and look at the gold-brushed cliffs. Hand-hewn windows and walls cling to the side of the cliff in a mesmerizing pattern.

I trace the shape of the cliff dwellings with my finger on the glass. "So magical."

"Not to the original Paix. It must have been rough camping there as compared to the Tunnel Cities. No technology. Primitive."

"But they are so . . ." I try to think of another word to describe what I see. Remnants of greatness is a phrase that comes to mind. The original dwellers had chosen to return to their lives in their primitive state after a brief diaspora into the modern world. They did not bring technology back with them. No government remembered they were even there. It is why they were spared by the Listener drones. Their language was unknown to any but their own.

"So what?"

Yet they had welcomed the Indigo Children—immigrants—into their homes, even though they were different. Words cannot describe how I Feel about the cliff dwellings. I finally say "magical" again.

"Still? How many times have we seen the cliff dwellings?"

"Not enough times," I say and continue to stare out of the window. "Admit that it is remarkable that someone has lived in the cliffs since well before the Paix."

"I do. There were humanoids within the cliffs before the Others. They are Ancient. And the Indentured live in them now. Direct descendants."

"The Indentured have carved out a place beneath the life that diminished. New feet in the footprints of life."

"What?"

"The footprints of life. The buildings, what is left behind. The things of life."

"Come on already," Mon says and pulls on my arm. "The cliffs are cool. I get that. So is racing. Except racing is much cooler."

"All right," I say and turn from the window. Several other Auraless are already engaged in the game, but there are two racing lanes left open. Mon picks the outside lane. I smile and follow her. She always picks the outside lane. Mon and I put on our gear in silence and watch them.

I am happy, thoughtless, until Mon says, "What do you think he will say at pow wow tonight?"

Pow wow follows every Assembly. It is more important, as it is just the Auraless who gather. I pull the racing goggles over my eyes. I Feel Mon's apprehension. I do not even want to think about pow wow. "Who?"

Mon makes a sour face. "Who? Ditero in a red Aura."

I laugh with Mon over the absurdity of that vision, then she continues. "You know who. Jaigon, your special friend who you take walks with early in the morning."

"I cannot attempt to fathom. He did not mention it to me."

"You squint when you lie."

I honestly do not know what Jaigon is going to speak about. "I am not lying."

Mon waves her right hand dramatically in front of my face like she is canceling my Words. "Fine. Hold it in. I will eventually get it out of you. Help me put the Caster on. Then I will help you."

I gather the strings of her Caster and tie them tightly around her. I am careful not to touch the sides. The material is sticky, as it is used to attract light balls.

Mon wraps the strings of my Caster around me. She ties it carefully to me. "You are so thin, I do not know if one of these would protect you from Impact. But you never hit Impact."

"One day, I will. And you are just as thin. When is the last time you ate non-supplementals?"

"Since we ate them together—too long ago. I am solid. Not thin."

"You are perfect."

"To you," Mon teases.

"To everyone." I hand Mon her goggles and head gear and point to the court. "Let us play."

Mon and I line up in the outside lane, and I tap my foot on the court. The court comes to life in a series of flashing colors. Mon steps on the Lift Board and taps her foot twice. The Lift Board rises, and she signals to the overhead Lexicon that she is ready to play by clapping her hands together three times.

The court starts to move. A single rope drops in front of me. Because we play at the maximum level, at least fifty light balls spin in the lane ahead of me. I take a deep breath, grab the rope, and start to run. The balls are made of lead but look alive in their light-coated casements.

The light balls react when Mon directs them with her eye

movements through the goggles. She relies on intuitive strategy determined by my body's trajectory and motion to place the light balls where my body will be.

The light balls spin and try to attach to my Caster. I duck to the right and continue running. The light balls sting when they attach, so I run, slide, and jump until I gain enough momentum to wrap myself around the rope and maneuver myself more quickly down the lane.

Several light balls attach to my breast plate. I brush them off with a violent arm sweep across my chest. I Feel how Mon will attack next, so I swivel to the right, then duck when a wave of light balls moves toward me.

Mon's attack is predictable, even if I was not a Feeler. "Always from the front," I mumble and lift my legs in tandem to avoid the next assault of light balls.

I grab onto the next rope when I see it and hoist myself up and over a pit of light balls on the floor. I wrap the rope around my feet and crouch until the end of the lane. I jump off in one fluid motion.

One light ball remains attached to me. I pick it off with both hands. The stinging sensation leaves as soon as I remove it.

"You are down to carrying only one," Mon says and steps off the Lift Board. She tears the goggles off her head and hops several times. The transition to firm ground is difficult after floating. "That is a personal best for you. Impressive."

"I think we play this game together too often. I anticipate what tactics you will employ." I watch as the light around the lead ball flickers and dims. I place it in the basin at the end of the lane. It stops glowing. It is plain and lifeless without the light.

"I change it up every time," Mon says and pats my shoulder. "You are a Feeler, so we do not play often enough. When you get through the course with nothing attached to the Caster, then we will have played you right into an Aura. My turn. Go easy on me."

"I am content with one carry," I say and step on the Lift Board. I double tap my foot on the floor. Mon taps her foot and gets a head start on the run. I adjust my goggles quickly, then center my balance on the Lift Board and pursue.

Controlling the light balls through the goggles is easy for me. So is anticipating Mon's defensive maneuvers. By the time we are halfway down the lane, Mon has six light balls lodged in her Caster. I am not concerned, as it takes twice that number for Impact. Impact is only a shock, and it will definitely not kill a Being. Impact does leave a sense of disorientation for several days, though, so no one wants to actually hit Impact.

I slow the Lift Board and direct the light balls to attack under Mon's flying body. She does not pick up on my offensive move fast enough. When she discovers the light balls attached underneath her, she sweeps them off with her left hand but misses the last rope and falls.

She rolls several times, but the light balls do not deactivate. Light balls move around the periphery of my vision. I train my eyes on the off circle in the corner of the screen and blink several times in succession.

Nothing happens.

More light balls attach to Mon. I blink furiously to shut the light balls off but cannot control them. I cannot count the number, but it is double that of Impact. Mon twists and turns on the floor, and I Feel her desperation keenly. I also Feel her pain.

Failure. Murder. Failure. Murder.

"Mon," I scream. I fly by her, jump from the Lift Board, and run to the control panel. I slam my hands down repeatedly on our play panel and finally crush the play goggles beneath my feet. The light balls stop. I fall when I turn around but push myself up to a run. I slide to a stop next to Mon. I bend down and rip light balls off her Caster. "Are you okay? Are you okay?"

Mon's eyes are frantic, and she clutches my arm. Once I remove enough of the light balls, she loosens her grip. "Yes. Get these off of me."

My fingers sting, but I keep pulling light balls off. "What happened?"

Mon shakes her head and closes her eyes. "It was like, all of a sudden, I saw more light balls than I have ever seen on the lane. It frightened me, and I had to get them off. But they would not come off. Did you do that?"

I shake my head no. I pull Mon to me and hug her fiercely. "I was only controlling five of them."

Mon hugs me back. "Only five?"

"Yes, I swear. I would never attack you like this. It hurts me when you are hurt. Are you injured anywhere?"

Mon stands up stiffly. "Just some bruising. Maybe a miscommunication in the program? But that is impossible. The Lexicon controls it."

I bite my lip and search in my Being, but do not Feel anything off. I did hear the voice, but I still do not know where it comes from. "Improbable. Not impossible."

"But the collective . . ."

I interrupt Mon. "Is not infallible, Mon. Maybe with the murder, things are not as focused for them. We have seen evidence of that today—missing lights, strange coloration. We cannot know how deeply this happening has disturbed their thoughts."

"Did you just say that the Paix is not infallible?"

"I did. Obviously. I would never hurt you."

"I know, I know," Mon says. "I do not doubt you. Come on, let's go."

We walk down the lane back to where the Casters are stored. No one bothers us, though I know that other Auraless saw what happened.

"I did not try to hurt youm," I say again and fold my Caster. I put it back into its container. I pick up the smashed goggles from the floor and place them in the Replicator. "No more racing."

"I really do believe you. I will report this in detail to Mechanical. And complain. Loudly."

I follow Mon out of the racing field. I Feel her suffering still, and I wish that I could not.

Failure? Disconnect? Why?

38

CHAPTER 4

Over the course of several spances, the Republic rebuilt their forces. The Triumphant spread its reach too far in empire building and became careless. Both factions built Fusion Reactors that they could not control. The Triumphant's first Fusion explosion destroyed most of the ancient continents of Asia and Europe. The Republic countered with a second, then third Fusion explosion which obliterated both continents from the Lexicon's maps. Fallout from the explosions damaged the reproductive capabilities of many remaining species. The Triumphant and the Republic effectively obliterated most life on Earth in the quest for domination.

—HISTORIES OF PAIX, INDIGO 2.3

SHAB, OUR EVENING MEAL, is normal. We dress in proper attire: long, white shirts over flowing pants of varying neutral colors. Braided, rainbow cords fall from our shoulders and tie loosely under our arms near the waist. They vary in length by our ages.

Mon, Par, and Vena speak about the day while I eat and listen to them. I envy their friendship, the way Words flow between them effortlessly. Because they are so close, I Feel their emotions even when I try not to, so I keep my distance.

The younger helds take away the plates and leftovers and return them to the Replicator for recycling. Tension is high in the room. I Feel that everyone is on edge and impatient.

Jaigon calls the pow wow after final Shab. We convene by age group in the Oratory area, the only place in the Koja where the Paix Lexicon is not present. The Oratory is bare of decoration. The ceiling is constructed in a series of non-glass materials for better acoustics. It has several rows of seating and an open space in the front where we give programs of dance, song, and drama at the end of our courses.

Jaigon looks slowly around the room before he speaks. He commands attention. "There is news. Another Auraless child has been delivered to the Yellow. He is now in the Kitalu."

The Auraless in charge of the younger helds whisper to each other. The Kitalu is already cramped, as all children under the age of six are cared for within its space.

"Resources will be diverted to the Kitalu for the Yellow child." Jaigon pauses. "A new room will be made available for sleeping quarters."

I swallow hard. Once we complete school at eighteen, we are assigned individual rooms. Which means Els's room will become a sleep area for our children now that she has Ceased. It is the only unused room at this time. The cycle of life continues whether we wish it to or not.

Jaigon continues. "We also have a child to be born amongst our own."

Utica and Suela stand. The Paix had not attended their Binding ceremony, but all of the Auraless had witnessed it. I had enjoyed watching their union.

"It is Recorded by the Auraless that this child shall be the first born amongst us," Jaigon adds. "This is the time for Dissention."

After a full minute of silence, Jaigon nods. "This news has been accepted."

All of the Auraless clap once in unison to indicate agreement. Utica and Suela sit down. Suela's mouth relaxes into a smile. I Feel relief and warmth around her, happiness. I Feel the second life within her. It is a flicker, a tiny speck of happy thought.

Jaigon raises both his arms. "We shall not share this news of progeny with the Paix yet due to the murder that has transpired. I ask now, in the sanctuary of our Oratory, has one of our own committed this crime against Els? Speak."

Silence. I Feel fear and hear murmurs of confusion around me. I look out the window at the sheer cliffs and the sea. Once, the sea was far away, as is recorded in the Ancient texts. I like the sea being close. The sound and motion are comforting to me, and I wish that I was swimming in it now.

Several Auraless speak at the same time. "What if Els was murdered by the Paix? What if another one of us is next? What if . . ."

Elias's voice cuts through them. "What if it was one of us?"

Jaigon raises his arms for silence. "This is not the time for Dissention or Accusation. I ask for a timeline."

A girl from the twelve held class raises her hand. She is soft spoken and very shy. Jaigon acknowledges her. "Ventra, Subject 109. Speak."

"I ask to Illuminate."

Jaigon raises both his hands palms up, indicating that Ventra should stand and address the gathering.

"Els engaged me in Aura building, as she is . . . was my Matching. She then left our Koja and told me she was visiting her parents. I did not follow, as I am only twelve held and cannot leave the Koja . . ."

Ventra begins to tremble. The bond between a younger held and their Matching is like that of siblings. Her loss Feels palpable to me. I do not have a Matching, as a Feeler would be detrimental to the emotional growth of a younger held.

Jaigon looks at Ventra with kindness. "In Singular. Understood." He motions for Ventra to sit. "This Illumination is helpful. We will assign a new Matching to you. Is this the last time Els was seen by the Auraless?"

No one else stands to Illuminate. Jaigon makes a complete circle around the room. His dark pants accentuate the power in his form. His eyes settle on the Chai. The Chai is our elected internal governing body. In the Ancient texts, Chai means life.

"Will the Chai stand?"

Seventeen Auraless stand. Jaigon makes the 18th member, our number for Chai. He raises his right arm and swings it in a circle. "Ditero communicated that the collective Paix does not tolerate murder. Els left our Koja for Paix and returned to us broken. Perhaps it is time to sever our connection to Paix."

Protests and cheers fill the room. I Feel the emotions in the room spike. My stomach turns.

Jaigon raises his arm and shouts three times. Everyone stops speaking. "I am asking for Consideration. It may be time to devise a new plan for our people."

"But we are all one people," I blurt out loudly.

"Murder has been committed, Subject 46," Jaigon responds. "Do you Illuminate?"

I stand. The room is spinning, and I stumble forward. "The Paix is our home, and they are our people. They have provided a system for us to live and prosper within. We cannot abandon them."

Several of the Chai nod their head in agreement with me. Jaigon does not. "Our history and present is written by the Paix's collective thought. But the future does not have to be. Explain this murder."

"There is no falsehood within the Paix. It is forbidden in the Laws to lie in the Koja. There is another explanation."

Jaigon makes a scoffing sound. "In truth, we do not know if they lie or they do not. We do not . . ."

Shalice, one of the eldest on the Chai cuts Jaigon off. She is serious and blunt, and her face is jagged. "Jaigon, do not forget your place as Leadership. All are allowed a voice."

"Do not Feel fear."

"But he is right," Joo-roo says clearly. "We do not communicate with them directly, so we cannot know if they are hiding Els's murder."

Joo-roo is my age. We share the same teaching wing. He helps the children with their ability to communicate feelings. Every third semester, we teach a joint class of Word and movement that I enjoy.

Jaigon turns his attention to Joo-roo. "Explain."

Joo-roo stands and faces the Chai. Joo-roo traces his family to the original cliff dwellers, and Auraed or not, he is proud of this. In honor of his heritage, he wears a loose-fitting Ancient robe for Shab designed after those of the original dwellers.

He moves his hands in the sign of peace. His robe flutters like a rainbow of moving colors. "We do not know how Els was eliminated, only that she was."

"I have inquired, and no one has claimed," Jaigon responds. "Do you have a better plan to find a murderer when there does not seem to be one?"

"I do. We are not privy to the mind of the collective Paix. But we do interact with its technology, extensions of the Ortus. The Ortus's programming is not capable of disseminating falsehood to the Lexicons."

The room is quiet.

"Then you maintain that it is one of our kind," Jaigon says.

"I move to consider a different angle."

Shalice nods. "This is logical reasoning. What are your thoughts?"

"Perhaps one of the Paix no longer complies with the collective," Joo-roo answers without hesitation.

I do not like Joo-roo's tone. Something is off about his Words. I cannot Feel his emotions. It is like a thick wall is around him. I have never encountered it before and wonder if he has been exercising his Talent in a different way.

Shalice clasps her hands in front of her chest. "This is an

interesting angle."

Joo-roo's voice shakes when he answers. "It is truth."

"We have no way to verify that," Jaigon says and motions for Joo-roo to sit down.

"Not so quickly," Heidig says. Heidig has never been friendly towards the younger helds, as his temperament is serious and he studies the Ancient texts. He is short and fair with thin fingers. "There is validity in his conjecture."

Jaigon frowns. "However interesting or valid your angle may be, a Paix cannot function in the Singular. His or her implants would not connect, and alone, he or she would Cease."

"It should be investigated," Heidig maintains. "Change does happen. Think of the new child to be amongst us."

"Agreed," Shalice says. "And if this angle does not prove to bear answers, what do you suggest, Jaigon?"

Jaigon clasps his hands behind his back and walks in a circle. "We know their history," Jaigon begins.

I stand and say loudly, "Our history."

Jaigon stops walking in circles and looks at me. "Consider the Tunnel People."

"They were not our kind," Heidig mutters.

Jaigon acknowledges Heidig, but continues. "I fear that elimination or forced removal of the Auraless is the next step for the Paix."

"These actions were taken against the Paix," I say firmly. "The Paix was the minority."

"They are not now," Sarta says. Sarta rarely says anything during pow wow, so when she does, the Auraless listen. She clutches the rainbow amulet around her neck. It is a circle of color around an implant encapsulated in clear glass, a gift from the Paix to the eldest Auraless. She always wears it. "The murder is irrelevant. There are two questions that must be answered. Do we continue to be a minority in the Paix, or the majority in our own community? Is a non-Paix supported community even possible?"

"We are not without knowledge," Jaigon comments.

Sarta smiles at Jaigon. She pats his arm fondly. "I did not say that we were. We would lose much and gain much with this change, if the Auraless vote for it. Shall we vote?"

Jaigon shares a glance with Sarta. "The vote will be cast to sever or remain. The rest of this discussion will continue at a later time. We will pause now for Consideration."

Sarta sits, and I watch the continued non-verbal exchanges between her and Jaigon. I Feel Jaigon's impatience and Sarta's calmness. It is an interesting mix.

Mon whispers to me, "Jealousy is not a pretty color on you. Will you vote to sever?"

"No. My parents are Paix. This is just reactionary. And I am not jealous."

"Jaigon. Reactionary?" Mon says sarcastically.

Failure. Disconnect.

My head feels like it is swimming in a murky ocean. The strange voice is louder, more demanding.

"Stop. Stop."

Failure. Disconnect.

The voice swells to a high pitch, and I think my mind may explode.

Sarta addresses the group. She touches her Paix necklace. "Let the younger helds go to their parents if they wish to. In two days, we will reconvene for a proper voting."

"It shall be done in this way," Jaigon says and marks the end of the pow wow with a final downward stroke of both hands.

The Auraless stand. We place our hands together in a triangle and bow our heads. The pow wow is complete.

Mon grabs my elbow. "I am already thinking less about voting and more about this weekend."

The voice dissipates from my mind. I breathe more easily. My vision is blurry, and I am grateful for Mon's hand on my elbow. "Let us not speak of it until we are on our way."

This weekend is a special festival in Paix—the Vociferone. It is held near the Ortus once a spance to celebrate Auraed culture.

Food, music, and dance fill the day. Our Paix families always attend it together.

Mon clenches her teeth and pretends she is carrying something very heavy. She pulls my arm towards her chest like I am stabbing her. "Don't. Be. Such. A. Downer."

"All right," I say and laugh. My vision clears. We turn down the hall to our room. Since our families live in the same Tether in Paix, we travel home together. It is one of the reasons we are so close. "Enough. Let us pack."

Mon prances in front of me, then puts both hands on the door and bangs her fists. "Let me in! Let me in!"

I step around Mon and place my hand on the scanning pad. Mon follows me inside when the door slides open. We choose clothes together and download the drawings that we have prepared for our families to our personal Lexicons. The drawings help us share our news.

"What if things are different now?" Mon says. "Since the murder."

It is rare that Mon is concerned about anything, so I know she is serious. I Feel her anxiety. "They will not be. Our parents will be the same. Do not forget your outer wear this time. The Replicated ones look terrible."

Mon retrieves her outer wear—special robes to wear at mealtimes in Paix. We hand-stitched them with the help of Lexicon diagrams. "What if we sever? It will be different then."

"Do you wish to leave this?" I ask and indicate the room. The room we share with Par and Vena is clean and purposeful. Space is managed efficiently. The windows open to the sea. "The majority will not wish to risk stability. This is home, and we have all that is required."

"Are we not going home now?"

"We can have more than one home, as we have more than one friend," I say softly and reach under the bed for my Paix shoes.

"But there is only one best, one true friend."

I know better than to argue with Mon. I never win. Instead,

I hold my Paix shoes to my chest. They are beautiful. I envision putting them on one day when my Aura appears and arriving at my parents' Tether. They would already know I was there.

"Without Words."

Mon puts her hand in front of my face. "Where are you? Hello? Drop the shoes."

I push Mon's hand away. I place my shoes under the bed and say, "Finding my Aura."

Mon makes a tsk-ing sound. "Find one for me while you are searching. Let us go. You know the Paix hates it when we are not on time."

I follow Mon down the hallway. Many Auraless are talking about the pow wow in the Salles and Calles. I Feel a scattered collection of emotion. It is hard to determine who Feels what when emotion is this high, as everyone Feels something.

I am glad when we leave the Koja—I do not want to think about the vote or sort through emotions. The day nears its closing. Only a few Auraless are walking to their traveling apparatuses. I count only ten that plan to visit their Paix family in the Go-Go's. The number lessens each spance.

All Paix travel in personal crafts, or as we call them, Go-Go's. They are round orbs with heated gas beneath them, so they float. They are see-through and have several white chairs and a console within. The navigation system is linked to the Ortus.

Once, we took a school trip to see the Ortus. The visit had disappointed me, as I believed the Ortus was an actual person, not a highly sophisticated, solar-powered, circuit collective brain. Each member of the collective transmits data from their implant above their right or left ear to the nearest Lexicon. Each Lexicon then transmits the data to the Ortus for processing and storage. Everything happens instantaneously. No data is ever lost. Everything is linked to the Ortus.

"Except us."

"Even the Indentured," I say bitterly. Connected by programming, they are like the Yuan and the Koja, reliant on the Ortus to keep them functioning. So are we, but not as closely. The Indentured receive programming modules at birth to correct birth defects and allow for productive lives.

"What about the Indentured?" Mon asks.

"Nothing," I mutter.

We reach our Go-Go. The Paix replicated several Go-Go's with manual inputs for us, and we share them. The Mechanical wing of the Koja is working on building our own, specialized Go-Go.

"What gives? You are too quiet."

"The new Go-Go," I say to Mon. "It will be different when we can program the Go-Go to travel to different places than Paix."

"What other place is there? The Moon?" Mon makes a dramatic face and points at me. "That is it! You want to go to The Moon!"

"The Moon was lost thousands of spances ago. If the Paix could not find it, then neither could I. Stop teasing me."

"Well, one can wish," Mon says and opens the bottom hatch by unlatching it. She secures the free end of it to the ground. Steps are carved into the surface. "Nice to see you, Martha. I will board now."

"She reminds me more of a Lola," I say and pat the Go-Go's side. I climb the steps and secure the hatch behind me. I select the address of our Strand from the six pictorial options while Mon dances around the enclosure.

"You seem happy," I comment as Mon falls to the Go-Go's floor and wiggles.

Mon gyrates on the floor for a few more minutes, then whistles. "A change of scenery is always good." She checks the inside door lever of the emergency exit and stretches her arms above her head. "Celebrating it is also good."

"To the Moon, or to Paix?"

"Paix first, then the Moon," Mon answers playfully.

I select the address again. It does not load. "Or nowhere. Something is wrong with the Go-Go."

"Let me try," Mon says and reaches over me. She is unsuccessful.

I initiate a complete restart sequence. A series of nonsensical dots crisscross the screen. "Wait with the Go-Go, and I will locate one of the Mechanicals. Continue to dance around it if gives you pleasure."

"I will gain Martha's cooperation. Are you going yet?"

"Yes, yes. I want to start the journey to Paix as much as you do."

I jog back to the Koja and take the shortcut across the flat front lawn. I want to see my parents and hope that the Go-Go's malfunction can be solved quickly. I turn the corner to the Mechanical entrance at top speed. I slide to a stop as Jaigon is waiting near the door. I slow to a walk and catch my breath.

"I believe you are returning two days on the prior," Jaigon says. "Or perhaps you have altered your choice?"

I can tell he is watching how I move when I stop in front of him. I feel a flush of heat rise in the pit of my stomach. I clear my throat. "Our Go-Go is inoperable. Mon is waiting with it."

Jaigon raises his eyebrows. "Interesting."

"It is unfortunate timing." I enter the Koja and force myself not to turn around in case he is watching. I know that we need to leave soon if we are to make Strand Time and see our parents. We will not be allowed entrance if we are past Strand Time. I walk a little faster.

Hasta is standing in front of the Mechanical door. His shirt is open in the front, and his wide pants look like sails on what the Ancients traveled the seas in. He is not my favorite person, but we are not enemies. He always looks at me like he is not quite sure how I function in my Being. "Hasta."

"Subject 46," Hasta replies.

I hate it when people call me by number, but I try not to let it show. "Our Go-Go, number 13 for our Unit, is inoperable."

"There are several Go-Gos down. Perhaps this delay allows you to consider the pow wow?"

I look at Hasta blankly.

"Come on, Subject 46. You cannot think these malfunctions are purely coincidental?"

I had not considered it. Jaigon's comment makes sense now. I stare at Hasta. He crosses his arms and makes a face. "You cannot always Feel. Sometimes, thinking helps."

I continue to stare at Hasta. Eventually, he breaks eye contact. "All right, Subject 46. Keep Feeling the edges. Let us do the thinking for you. Go wait by your Go-Go. The Mechanicals are making rounds to repair the disfunction even as we parlay."

"Mon is waiting with the Go-Go."

Hasta smiles. "Then perhaps I will personally take care of the aberration."

I hesitate. "Why do you dismiss my Talent?"

Hasta raises his eyebrows. They are bushy, and the effect gives him a surprised look. "I do not. I ask that you consider adding thought to your decision-making process. Balance."

"Partings," I say quickly and walk away. I do not have time to listen to Hasta. The Koja is unsettled. The colors around me are not genuine. Everything feels a little too crisp, like I'm looking through a sharply-focused hole at a room that is spinning.

Someone calls my name, and I wave in the direction of the sound but continue to walk down the hallway out of the Koja and directly to Mon. Mon is dancing maniacally around the Go-Go and chanting.

"Trying the Ancient ways on it," Mon explains when I approach. She keeps spinning. "Hoping for a healing."

I motion for Mon to follow me. We leave the craft in front of the Koja and head into the woods that frame our Koja on three sides.

Mon catches up to me. "Are you trying this again? I was really starting to Feel something back there, pushing my Aura. So this had better be good."

"Yes," I say and walk until we get to the stone circle. "It had better be."

I raise my arms. I have been getting closer to understanding the Paix collective. When I Drift, the Paix look like tiny lights too far away for me to reach. I Feel their presence like strings and know when the Paix consciousness shifts.

It is shifted now. Something in the Auraed world is off, and it creates imbalance. Colors are off, glitches in programming—like the light balls. It could be a simple issue. With the newest yellow child born Auraless, it may be too many female or male within the Paix, or not enough children in one Strand. Or it could be the murder.

"I was on to something back there. I felt light as a feather."

I look at Mon curiously, as whenever I have been in the presence of the collective, I have noticed the exact opposite. Everything seems heavier. "You Feel an imbalance, just as I do. I Feel it as darkness. Heaviness."

I enter the circle. Mon huffs and sits down on one of the viewing rocks in the clearing. She sighs. "Fine. I will wait. Stand guard. Watch. Whatever you need, Lisle. I am a giver."

I smile at Mon, as I rely on her loyalty, even when she does not want me to. I stand in the middle of the circle and focus. I shut the world off and look with different sight at the inside of my own tissue, at my own fabric. I take a deep breath and let my mind Drift.

I find the strings of the collective hovering closer than before. There is a buzzing noise surrounding me. The strings begin to wrap around my wrists. I shift my weight to the right, then the left. A sharp pain in my mouth holds me still, like a specimen.

I cry out. I am falling.

I wake up in my parents' home. My Father is standing over me. He smiles at me when I open my eyes. "What happened?"

My Father seems to understand, which surprises me, as I spoke in Words. "How did I get here?"

He holds up three pictures that he has drawn. In the first picture, I am unconscious in the stone circle. In the second, I am floating in space near the Moon. In the third, I am lying in my bed.

"I floated through space? Ancient space?"

My Father covers his ears. I reach out to touch his face, but he catches my hand and puts it back by my side. His face looks distorted, out of shape. He draws a picture of me floating and other bodies connecting to my mind. I nod. "Yes, I was trying to connect."

Father nods his head. He points to his ears and then touches my forehead. I shake my head, as I do not understand. "Did I connect? Could you hear me?"

Mother comes into my room and puts her hand on my Father's shoulder and squeezes. She beckons to me with her right hand, and I sit up in bed. She points to her eyes with her right index finger and blows me a kiss.

"I know what your eyes look like. It is your Aura."

My Father touches my lips with his fingers and then brings his fingers up to his head. A metal plate forms across his forehead, then disappears. I am shocked. "Father?"

"It is what you have seen," Father replies. His voice is a great echo in my mind. He closes his eyes and opens his hands the way the Auraed do in Personal Time, when they share all of their thoughts and feelings with the Ortus.

Mother joins him, and I stand up. I do not grasp exactly what is happening, but I Feel strongly that my parents want me to try to connect with them. I have never been able to Feel anything from my parents.

I mimic their posture and close my eyes like I do in the stone circle. I find the strings of light that dance around me, just out of reach. A sliver like a knife cuts through my awareness.

I hear what I think is my Father's voice murmuring in my mind. "Struggle. There is one from you of the old Paix, a virus in the collective. Singularity. The Ortus cannot control the new, the old. System failure."

"Father, I . . ."

My mouth moves soundlessly as if I now see through my

Father's eyes. My Mother presses her face to my hand. It is cold, like metal. My Father's voice murmurs through my mind with the weight of six million voices.

"System failure. Program. Rest."

The weight is too much. I put my hands over my ears and scream.

CHAPTER 5

. . . most of the remaining Ancient nations evacuated underground into the Tunnel Cities. They were led by the Indigo Children, our distant ancestors, who survived the Fusion Wars because of their unique communication skills. They developed a collective conscious-ness and did not need Words to speak. Their silence kept them safe.

—HISTORY OF PAIX, INDIGO 3.1

"WHAT ARE YOU DOING?" Mon's voice is high. I Feel her terror. "You asked me to sing, then you fell down. It was weird because I know you hate distractions when you are doing this."

"Where are my parents?"

"In their house, I assume." Mon kneels beside me. "Where we are not. Stop being so dramatic. It is eerie."

"I am not being dramatic." My head clears, and I study Mon. Her color is normal. I look around the stone circle clearing, then further into the surrounding forest. The colors are crisp, edges defined. I no longer Feel disoriented.

"You are acting like one of them."

"There is a problem in the Paix. I think my parents . . ."

"What are you doing out here?" Jaigon's voice booms over the clearing.

"Lisle passed out. She was trying to connect. One minute, she was standing, and then next . . . out on the ground. Visions of the Paix."

"Not visions. Words from my Father. We need to go to Paix. Now."

Jaigon kneels next to Mon so he is almost level with me. He looks deep into my eyes, then licks his lips. I Feel concern radiating from him, and something else.

"Ask her why she wanted me to sing," Mon says and looks from Jaigon to me. "She never answered me."

"It helped me hear through the echo."

Jaigon touches my cheek. "Echo? Did you connect?"

I shake my head no. "No, but it was different—like looking at yourself in a reflective surface. I was in my room in Paix, and my Father told me about a virus in the collective. He called it a Singularity, old and new. The Orzus cannot control it."

"A virus?"

"He said virus and system failure. The tone was urgent. There is danger. The colors are off. Were off—they are back to normal now. But the danger is still there."

"What kind of danger?" Mon asks.

"His Words were garbled."

Jaigon presses. "Try to make them sensibly consecutive for us."

"There is one from you of the old Paix," I repeat. "That is what he said in the dream. Then he said there was a virus in the collective, a power struggle. He mentioned a system failure and a program."

Jaigon shakes his head. "A power struggle is not a virus, it is simply against the collective mentality. And what system?"

"I know," I say miserably. I Feel Jaigon's indecision. "It is hard to sort out, but that is what he said. There is one from you of

55

the old Paix. Rest. And my Mother touched me, but she felt like metal."

"Ooh," Mon says. "I cannot imagine your Mother like that. What kind of metal?"

"That is unimportant," Jaigon says. "What did his Words mean to you?"

I know the answer; I heard it in my Father's head. "Failure."

"Old, new … but it is not you."

"No. But I have heard another voice. It tells me to disconnect, leave, depart."

Mon puts her hand on my forehead. "Another voice?"

I push her hand away. "I am fine. It is not Paix. I do not know what it is."

"Perhaps this Singularity?" Jaigon asks. "For how long?"

"Since the Assembly."

Jaigon looks serious. "You should have reported it."

"I did not know what it was to report. I still do not."

Jaigon accepts my explanation. "Do it again."

"Do what?"

"Drift. We need more information."

"It is not like that," I counter. "I am a stone in a pool of water. I Feel the ripples, yet I know that there is a vast body of water around me."

"I do not need specifics. Drift again and try to get some Feeling for this virus, the interloper, anything. The pathway seems open to you in this moment."

Jaigon is right. I walk to the center of the clearing and kneel. I focus my thoughts and find the silver threads. My body becomes weightless, then very heavy. I cannot move. I sink under a vast weight that knows no beginning or end. Time and space close in, and I cry out before I hit the wall looming in front of me.

My tongue is on fire, and my body wrapped in flames. I am trapped, immobile. I open my eyes in horror. I am wrapped in a blanket and in bed. I look around and recognize stacked, glass cubes. I am in the Healing at the Koja.

"Thank you for finally waking up."

I focus on the face. It is Mon. Her almond-shaped eyes are large. She blinks several times. "You went into a shaking fit and spoke a lot of gibberish. Then you passed out."

I touch my head gingerly because it is painful. I stretch my fingers and toes just to make sure that they are there. I do not recognize anything abnormal within my Being. "Gibberish about what?"

"About Auras and how the collective was a dead wall of bones. You hit it."

I cannot see Jaigon from the bed, but I recognize his voice. "You also said there was no collective, no Paix, just silence in a great darkness where once there was light. Then you collapsed and vomited. Mon and I carried you here."

"Mostly Jaigon," Mon explains. "I just kept your hair out of your face."

"Thank you."

Jaigon continues. "You have been asleep here for over two hours."

I struggle to move. Everything aches. Jaigon is sitting in an S-shaped, clear chair by the door. Joo-roo is to the right of Jaigon.

"I heard that you were knocking on the Aura's door," Joo-roo says softly. He walks to my bedside with his hands in his pockets. His face radiates concern. The wall I noticed within him earlier is gone, but something is different. I decide not to discuss it in front of the others.

I already do not feel as heavy as when I first regained Being. But I do Feel a residual sense of urgency. "Seems I ran into quite a door. Hard. A message is clear that all is not well. Have you contacted Ditero? The Paix?"

Jaigon looks over my head at the wall. "Negative to all. I believe you, however. All of the Go-Gos have malfunctioned. The Lexicon is down in most departments."

"It is an opportunity," Joo-roo says enthusiastically. "It is long overdue that we decide as a people about our need for a relationship, or lack of relationship with the Paix."

"Right now, we will watch and wait," Jaigon says. "No one will enter, and no one will exit. All of the Auraless are accounted for. If the Go-Gos and Lexicons do not return to functioning tomorrow, then we will begin an investigation outside of the Koja."

"But that may be too late."

"For now, we investigate within the Koja. Is your Being functioning again in normality?"

"Yes." Concern wraps Jaigon's emotions; I Feel it, but I cannot separate concern for me from concern for the Auraless.

"It is well, then," he says and stands. He turns sharply and walks out of the room. He does not say parting Words to any of us.

Mon sticks her tongue out. "He makes me uncomfortable."

"He is uncomfortable," Joo-roo says and steps closer to my bedside. "Your color is improving."

"Good. Normal color, I guess."

"You have not suddenly come by an Aura," Mon says. "If that is what you are asking."

I Feel that she is nervous. "Foolish wish."

"I wish we were not here," Mon continues. "We will miss the Vociferone."

"Me, too." I fondly think of our first Vociferone and how we danced and danced to the music. Mon and I had chattered all day and night, and the Paix seemed not to care that Words were flowing in their midst.

"I am happy staying right here," Joo-roo says. "My parents do not even notice when I am in the same Tether."

"Of course, they do," I say. I Feel the hurt in Joo-roo's Being. It is hazy, and I still Feel something off within him. "It is just hard for them. You have parents that are both of Orange Aura, correct?"

"Bright Orange."

"Hard to focus, but full of doing," Mon says in a mechanical voice. "I still remember that chart we committed to memory when we were but six spances."

"We all do," Joo-roo says. "Give me a color, and I will tell you their traits. Each and every one."

Joo-roo's tone is bitter. I lighten the mood. "Some other time. Your parents are probably trying to repair the Lexicon as we speak."

"Because they do not," Joo-roo says, then laughs at his own joke.

Joo-roo's emotions shift. He Feels right again. I am happy. "No bad humor in the Healing."

Neither of my friends pay any attention to my request. Joo-roo and Mon trade off less humorous one-liners about the Paix for a few more minutes.

My mind returns to heaviness. I replay the sequence of my Father's Words. They do not fit together. "What do you think he means, within? Does the collective mind even know what without feels like?"

No one answers me. I am Drifting . . .

Rest.

My dreams are gentle, and I wake feeling refreshed. A strange question fills my thoughts. Do my parents dream? There is no way to ask them if the collective dreams together or separately, or at all. I miss my parents, as I have seen them every weekend without fail since I relocated to the Koja.

The Healing is deserted. There is no one Auraless assigned to the Healing, as this Talent has not grown strong in the Auraless yet. A few have natural healing abilities, and they plus the Replicators have sufficed for our medical needs so far.

I stretch my arms above my head. The room is dark, and I push the blanket off. My shoes are by the bed, so I put them on and walk to the window. There is a strange quality to the dark outside, like it is moving. I touch the glass. It is warm. The stars are bright, and the cliffs are sharp and geometric.

"Oh," I exclaim. An Indentured male ambles across my line of vision. He is heading to the opposite end of the Koja. His gait is unsteady. He does not see me, and I step away from the window. I am glad that our sleeping and cleansing stations are made of white walls. I would not want to sleep or perform daily Ablutions surrounded by glass. There is no privacy.

The hour is late for an Indentured to be functioning. I return to my bed, but decide to report the sighting to Jaigon. It should be investigated. The door to the Salle is on the far side of the Healing. I wait in front of the scanning pad, palm up, but it does not recognize my presence. The door remains shut.

"This is not normal," I mutter. "Lexicon?"

The Lexicon in the center of the Healing station is like all the others in the Koja. It does not answer me, but the screen lights up. It is divided into a series of lines and squares and contained in a portable, rainbow-colored, three-dimensional box. I wipe my hand across the screen carefully. I am not recognized.

I shiver and realize that I am cold. I do not ever remember being in an uncomfortable temperature, as the central Lexicon manages the temperature throughout the Koja for our optimal comfort.

Perplexed, I return to the door and place my hand firmly on the scanning pad. It slides open quickly this time. I step forward with purpose to exit, but it slides closed before I am through. Surprised, I freeze and expect the door to open when it senses my presence. The pressure increases on my left arm and shoulder. I push my body through the opening. The door shuts noisily behind me. I rub my arm. It will bruise.

The hallway is eerily quiet and cold.

"Investigate."

I walk calmly down the Calle to the nearest Salle. There are no lights following me on the wall. The Salle is dim, and the temperature remains cool. I turn right and continue toward the Salon. It is empty. Several of the glass panes are cracked in the dome. The ceiling Lexicon flashes inconsistently between blue, red, and yellow.

I am completely alone. I begin to understand why my parents do not try to disconnect from the collective Paix. It is an unpleasant sensation.

"I would not try it, either."

I make my way to the center hall where the wheel of the Auras is imprinted on the floor, and I shout, "Greetings." My voice echoes around the high ceiling.

There is no reply, so I head down the Salle, turn into my Calle, and wind around the corridor to my room. I place my hand on the scanning pad. It opens. I step through quickly and keep my arms by my sides.

The room is empty. Mon's pack is not on the hook above her bed, and neither are the ones belonging to Par and Vena. My stomach clenches. I look out of the small window above our beds at the sea. I sit on my bed and stare at the wall. The room grows increasingly cold, and I cross my arms in front of my chest. "They have left me."

Failure.

Disconnect. Leave. Depart.

Where am I?

"Stop," I say firmly and stand up. The door shuts. I ignore the three distinct voices and fill my pack with things that I would not choose to leave behind: my personal Lexicon that connects me to my parents via visual imaging, a collection of ephemera from my spances at the Koja, and two Histories that my father has given me in Paix language.

I reach beneath the bed for my final treasure. My Paix shoes. They were made by my Mother's hands in rainbow colors. Each stitch represents the hope she has that I will gain an Aura. The design is sewn in red, the color of her Aura. I hold them to my chest for a moment, then place them carefully in the top of my pack. I close it and tie it tightly. Some things should never be lost. Or forgotten.

I hear a scratch on the door. I put the pack on my back and

position myself directly in front of the entrance pad. "Who requests entrance to these quarters?"

There is no reply, but I hear more scratching followed by a whine. Looking around the room, I can find no weapon to defend myself with.

"Stop this," I tell myself. I have no enemies and no need for a weapon. I take a deep breath and push the button for the door to open.

It opens immediately, and I stare into empty space. Something hits my knees. I ball my hands into fists to strike out, but stop before I scream as I thankfully look down first.

A sense of peace floods my mind when I recognize the Being clinging to my legs. Subject 142 reaches both hands up to me. His hair is spiky golden and his eyes hazel. He is small for his age and did not adjust well to the Kitalu. He is dressed in his sleeping skin—a tight-fitting, woven cloth garment. It is rainbow colored, as mine was when I was in the Kitalu.

I Feel the tendrils of his emotions, and they are full of fear. Zaron is like me, a Feeler. Though we do not connect, we have a general sense of the mood of each other. I channel pleasant thoughts so that he is reassured by my demeanor. Swimming in the sea, Jaigon . . .

"Zaron," I say softly and offer Zaron my hands. "You scared Lisle."

Zaron takes my right hand and then my left into his own. He makes a gurgling noise and stamps his foot. His face contorts. I lean over and pick him up. "You are just a two held. Why are you unaccompanied? Did you Feel Lilse's presence?"

The temperature of the room fluctuates. It is stifling hot. Zaron begins to cry. "Use your Words, Zaron. We have them to speak with," I chide and step through the doorway while I still can. The door does not shut on us, but it does not close behind me.

"Where are the others?" I ask. "Lisle was asleep. Now that she is awake, she must find the others."

Zaron puts his hand on my face. I Feel his confidence in me. I force myself to remain calm. "Where is your pack? Your Keep Safe?"

Zaron puts his head on my shoulder. I Feel confusion and sleepiness grip him. He will be of little help to me in deciphering what has happened.

I walk down the Salle to where the two helds live with their Keep Safes in the Kitalu. The lights are completely out, and when I try to open Zaron's door with the scanning pad, it is unresponsive.

"Will Zaron try?" Zaron does not answer me. He is asleep. I want to sit down and wait for help, but now there is more to think of than just myself. Determined, I walk back to the Salon, then past it to the Room of Administration. The Paix bring newborn Auraless to this office. All lineage records are inputted into the Auraless Lexicon here. There is also a store of items for new Auraless inside. I place my hand on the scanner, and the door opens. I enter but make sure Zaron's head is protected in case the doors shut on us.

The doors remain open. Everything is rainbow-colored in the room except the desk, which is clear. The lights and temperature control are functioning, as is the Lexicon. The screen is a maze of colored lines and shapes. I scan my wrist. I am recognized. My name and number appear on the screen.

"This is normal," I say and walk to the lockers. I search through the main locker with my right hand and hold Zaron in my left arm. I pull out a heavy, white shirt for Zaron and a rainbow blanket.

"These will do." I gently pry Zaron from my shoulder and set him on the ground. The child wakes. When I show him the shirt, he puts his hands up. I slip it over his head and say "shirt" in a quiet voice.

"Shirt," Zaron tries to repeat. His Word sounds more like "shrr," but I am pleased that he is responding to me. "Cold."

"Yes, I know. The shirt will help keep you warm." I open my

pack and tuck the blanket around my Paix shoes. I move to the next locker and find several supplemental packs. I put them on top of the blanket in my bag, then close it.

"Just in case," I say in a light voice when I notice Zaron watching me. He grabs onto my leg. I pat his head and smile at him. I walk with Zaron attached to my leg to the Lexicon. I touch the screen. It is now unresponsive. After several more attempts, it finally opens, and I touch the image for History.

Nothing appears.

Fear rises another notch within me, but I push it down. Zaron reaches for me, and I pick him up. "We must leave now, Zaron."

Zaron settles on my hip and wraps his arms around my neck. I Feel his contentment. I walk to the door. It opens for me and shuts behind me. The uncomfortable temperature outside of the room is immediately apparent. I grit my teeth and walk to the nearest Koja exit.

"Why did they leave us?"

When the exit door does not open at our presence, I begin to truly Feel despair. I take a deep breath and walk purposefully to the other end of the Salon. When the exit door does not open, I strike the scanning pad with my open palm.

The door cracks open. I turn to the side and hurry through. It shuts behind us with a final, dull thud.

I press my back against the Koja. The world is dark and cold. The air is wet—rain. It pours from the sky wildly, like the Earth is crying. It moves down my arm in rivulets. Each drop pools momentarily on my skin. Never have I seen or experienced rain like this. It normally only rains gently when the ground is too dry and needs nourishment. "Rain," I whisper in awe.

I juggle my pack and Zaron so that I can take the blanket out. I place the blanket over Zaron's head and wrap it around his body. I close my pack with one hand and shake Zaron gently with the other. "Zaron. It is raining. You must see."

The wind whips around me. Zaron turns in my arms and

whimpers with cold. He does not wake. My eyes fill with tears, and I let him sleep. "Why have they left us behind? We must find shelter and the others. But where?"

I look around the clearing. I cannot tell exactly what hour it is, but it is late, past sleeping hours. I take a step forward when the rain sounds less fierce. The Earth moves beneath me. I slip, and my weight makes an awkward impression in the ground. "It is like the Earth is alive."

I open myself to Feel, as it is the only way I can find the others. But instead of the Auraless' emotions, I see the threads of the Paix in my mind. The buzzing sound I heard before surrounds me.

I follow the threads toward the stone circle. The journey is slow, as my feet continue to sink into the ground. I eventually find the path that is the least soaked, use it as a guide, and move forward.

The buzz is louder now, but the Paix fades from my perception. I Feel the presence of emotions like mine more keenly. I make it to the center of the stone circle and Feel the presence of fear, love, and humor encircling me, but see no one.

"Greetings," I scream. The rain is coming down hard again. There are small pebbles of ice in it that sting when they strike my flesh. I shield Zaron's head with my free hand.

I look around the circle desperately. I Feel the Auraless are close. I shout, "Why do you hide?"

Zaron wails.

"Greetings! Greetings!"

I scream the Word mentally several times and try to find the ends of the tendrils of minds that I Feel moving around me. They have to answer me.

"Greetings, you have left me. Zaron as well."

I begin to shake. I know that as the cold and rain increases, our chances of survival decrease if I cannot find shelter for us. "The Koja, Paix. Options."

I consider both choices. I cannot go back to the emptiness of the Koja, and I know I will not make it to Paix on foot in freezing rain with the child. I turn within the circle and try to think of a third option.

"Everything is connected. Except us."

Zaron's sobs trigger a memory from the history of the first Paix when they found the cliffs. "We will find cover within the trees. Some are empty within. Hush now."

Zaron continues to cry. He holds part of my wet hair between his hands and pulls. "We will find cover within the trees. I will find the one that we can be safe within," I say soothingly. "Stop now."

Zaron cries louder and tries to make a Word, but his tongue fails him. Ice sticks to his eyebrows. "Do not cry so," I whisper to him and look at the trees around the circle. I move from the center of the stones and walk toward the largest tree. "This one. It will shelter us."

I step carefully across the slick Earth. I repeat "do not cry so" over and over to Zaron, when the ground gives way beneath us.

If I scream, I do not hear it. Perhaps it is in my mind only. Zaron holds onto my shoulders and laughs. I wonder who will bring me to the sky in Ritual, if Zaron has truly felt life during the shortness of his time, and finally, if Zaron's parents will blame me for his death.

CHAPTER 6

For many years, the Tunnel Cities flourished. The cities on the surface were presumed dead. Peace reigned as supreme Law of the land. The Leadership, a democracy representing all segments of the underground population of Nations, including the Faction Free, sent drone expeditions to the light every ten years. The images transmitted back to the Tunnel Cities were of residual poison gas and wild weather. No drone ever came back.

—HISTORIES OF PAIX, INDIGO 3.1

S TONE-SIZED SPHERES filled with a jelly-like substance break our fall. I struggle to keep Zaron in my arms as we sink deeper into the spheres. Our downward descent slows, then stops. The spheres surround us, and I feel like I am drowning. I clutch Zaron to me and push upward with my legs.

A voice calls my name. I am Drifting. I listen.

Disconnect. Leave. Depart.

I feel the edge of a consciousness that is vast. I am but a small drop in an ocean of time. The ocean turns into my parents' Strand and Tether on fire.

"NO!"

Disconnect. Leave. Depart.

Zaron cries.

"Focus. Escape."

I thrash my free arm around until I find the edge of the trench. I close my hand around a metal rung. I feel for a higher rung. When I find it, I hook my left hand around it and pull us up. Zaron is in my right arm. I pull and repeat the same motion over and over. Hands push through the surface of the spheres. They drag us from the trench. I clutch Zaron to me.

"Lisle," Mon cries and throws her arms around us. "I knew you would find us!"

I push Mon away and look around the room dazedly. We are underneath the ground. Gray metal surrounds us. There are no windows, no glass. The lights are recessed and replicated to look like the ones in our Salles, but the light they emit is dingy. The air smells stale and earthy.

I look up. The trench of spheres which softened our fall is directly below a three-foot-wide chute which we must have accidentally fallen through. Mon drapes a blanket round my shoulders. It is coarse and dark. "Why did you leave us in the Koja?

Mon's eyes fill with tears. I hear Zaron's name shouted. A woman pushes through the crowd. Zaron cries out to her.

"Zaron," she whispers and puts her arms around the child.

I instinctively hold the child closer. "Why..." I trail off when I Feel the love she has for the child. I recognize her as one of Par's companions. Her hair is distinctively red. She is Zaron's Keep Safe. But he should not have been abandoned. "Helga. He was left alone in the Koja."

"Please, my gratitude," she says desperately. I let her take Zaron from me. I Feel her relief. She cradles the child and sings a silly song about the color wheel. Zaron stops crying. She disappears with him into the crowd.

Silence fills the room now that Zaron's cries have stopped. I examine the faces around me. I know everyone, and they know me. "Why were we left at the Koja?"

Jaigon pushes through the crowd and pulls me to him force-fully. I Feel intense heat and a depth of caring that frightens me. I almost bring my arms around him, but he pushes me away before I can. "The doors kept you and the child captive."

"You left us. You left me."

"Apologies. We retreated here because we had to."

"You had to leave?"

"The climate control failed. It became difficult to breath as oxygen was not being pumped into the Koja. The doors would not open for us to rescue you and Zaron. Mechanical determined that everything else in both areas were functioning, so we evacu-ated. They are devising a scheme to override the Lexicon now, though it is not necessary since you have escaped. Please, feel welcomed."

I am in a box of metal. It is not comfortable or welcoming. The walls surrounding me are bare and base. The Auraless's emo-tions vacillate between anger and hope, fear and mistrust. There are too many gathered, too many emotions in a small space.

"She is in shock," Mon interjects. "I cannot imagine how she feels. She woke up alone. Let me bring her to the cleansing station."

Jaigon reaches for me. I move away. With so much emotional input, I cannot process physical contact.

Mon understands. "You can speak to her later. She has a lot to process right now."

Jaigon opens his arms shoulder height, palms up in the Paix gesture of acceptance. "We did not leave you. The Koja wanted to keep you."

I clasp my hands in front of me and close my eyes. I forgive Jaigon. When I open them, Jaigon is gone. Mon leads me down a hall. Bars run across the ceiling, and the walls are made of scratched, metal sheets. Many Auraless hands touch my arm as I pass them. I Feel their support and awe. I do not flinch, but I have no Words to say.

Disconnect. Leave. Depart.

I shake the voice out of my head. Mon is speaking to me.

"... was not an easy choosing. Jaigon had to order Helga to leave without Zaron. No one wanted to leave you, either, but the Salon filled with vile-smelling smoke, and the rain began outside in earnest. The Salles were bitterly cold, and the Calles burning up. It was like the oxygen was being sucked out of the Koja. Jaigon feared for our safety and had to ..."

Mon's Words stream across me. I interrupt, "Wait. Smoke was filling the Koja?"

Mon opens a door to the left in the hallway. "Smoke came from several of the Replicators. It smelled foul."

The next passage is narrow and dark. The walls are stone and a little damp when I touch it. I do not like their texture. "I have never seen a Replicator malfunction."

"No Being has." Mon slides the next door open. "We have to manually open the doors in this shelter. It is like a maze."

"And we are lost in it?"

"No. We are the newest occupants finding our way in it."

Mon's optimism is tangible—and I do not need to Feel it to know it is there. But a sense of oppression overwhelms me. The walls in this room are dark. Strange cups hold lights with an odd glow. The doors are not curved, but square. Beams connect to the ceiling in strange angles. Pipes run from the floor like veins. There are no colors anywhere—just oppressive gray. And there is no Lexicon. "What is this place? We are caged in, trapped."

Mon takes the pack off of my back and rests it on a long, rectangular bench. She hands me a towel. "Do not be so dramatic. This is the cleansing station. Showers, Ablution receptacles. If you mean the entire shelter, Jaigon led us here. It is beneath the Ancient stone circle."

"My circle of stones."

"The Ancients', really. They are the ones who moved the stones, made the circle. You have just adopted them. Jaigon told us that the technology is consistent with that of the Befores.

The shelter was constructed perhaps during their Fusion Wars. He found it by accident over a year ago and prepared it for the Auraless."

"Then it is . . ."

"Human-made. All of the technology is obsolete, but was easily repairable or updated, thanks to Mechanical. Jaigon stocked it with the help of the Koja Replicators."

There are four, thin metal lockers against the far wall labeled Top, Bottom, Underly, and Overly. There are adequate towels and a stock pile of soaps and other necessaries for Ablution on several shelves next to the lockers. "He knew . . ."

"He anticipated. He is Leadership."

"He replicated all of this?"

"He and Sarta did. Some of the other oldest helds. It is impressive."

I pick a sliver of soap out and put it into the pocket of my pants. I open the locker labeled Top. I choose a shirt in the right size, then appropriate matching sizes from the other three lockers. None of the clothing is the same. "These are darker than our normal clothing. More earthen. And each one is Singular. Not Paix styling at all."

Mon is quiet. She is watching me, and I Feel uncertainty in her Being. "What?"

"How did you know where we were? You and Zaron fell right through the trap door. Jaigon fell through by chance."

"Is that what you call it?" I say wryly and walk into the first stall to the right of the lockers. "A trap door?"

"That is what Jaigon calls it."

I take the soap sliver out of my pocket, then take off my soiled clothes. I look for a Replicator, but do not find one. I place the dirty clothes outside of the shower. "No Replicator, right?"

"No. Everything has to be washed. I suspect Jaigon has a plan for that, too. But how did you know the trap door was there? That we were here?"

"I could Feel the presence of emotion." A series of knobs are in front of me. I turn the knob closest to me to the left. The water is lukewarm, but not unpleasant. "I followed it."

"You adjust the temperature with the knobs. Jaigon explained when we arrived."

I turn the knob further to the left and am rewarded by stinging hot water. The throbbing pain in my shoulder and arm begin to recede. I complete Ablutions and breathe deeply. After several extra rinses, I sigh and turn the water off. "Left the towel."

"But you could not hear our thoughts?" Mon asks anxiously. "Here."

Mon throws a towel over the stall door, and I catch it. I dry off and wrap the towel around me. "The water is different," I say and slip into my new clothes quickly. They are not sized like my Paix clothing. The shirt and pants fit more precisely to my form. "These are strange."

Mon makes a pained noise like a low hum. "Come on. Could you hear our thoughts?"

"Not your thoughts. And honestly, I felt the collective more than the Auraless. It was a coincidence I found the trap door."

Mon is right in front of the stall door when I open it, and our noses almost touch. I look into her eyes, and they are beautiful and dark, depthless.

"You would not lie to your best friend, would you?"

"No." I step around Mon. "You would not let me."

"True."

Mon hands me a pair of shoes that look like glass. They are soft and pliant, rubbery. I slip them on my feet. They fit. "I like these. More roomy."

"And not rainbow colored. I did not realize how much I have come to dislike rainbows. Solids for me from now on."

I raise my eyebrows. The presence of color has always been part of our lives. The change in Mon's opinion is drastic. Without the rainbow, I am not sure what day it is—what to eat, how to think. "Well, there are no rainbows here. How long have you been in this shelter? What is it called?"

"Jaigon and the Mechanical just call it Under Stone, so I guess that is what we will all call it. We evacuated three hours ago. Jaigon had just approved a plan for you and Zaron to be rescued when you fell into us. There was a lot of excitement."

I run my hands through my hair. "Do we have a . . ."

"Jaigon did not think about that. Let me help."

Mon runs her fingers through my hair, and together we get most of the tangles out. "You said there was excitement. I did not Feel that."

"Fear. No one knew what was going to happen, and then you found us."

"Yes. But you already seem comfortable with these new facilities. Why would there be fear?"

"New surroundings. Lots of questions."

"It seems placid now. I do not Feel anything out of the ordinary."

"Jaigon gave us a detailed orientation. It makes sense in a grid-like way. It is not unlike the Koja."

"This is not the Koja."

"No," Mon agrees. "Definitely not."

The door swings open, and Hasta stands in the doorway. "Jaigon wants to see Lisle."

I feel Hasta's eyes roll over me, then Mon. In the new clothes, I feel more naked. Because the material stretches closely to my skin, I feel like Hasta is staring directly at my body. "All right. Stop staring."

"These clothes suit you," Hasta says.

"Gratitude." I scoot around him.

"What about me?" Mon asks.

"You, too. Especially you."

Mon giggles and links her arm with mine in the hallway. We pass several middle helds. They stare at me. Mon whispers in my ear, "Now that you are so popular, do not forget the little people."

"I am not popular. Hasta is a flirt."

"I mean everyone else." Mon winks at me and squeezes my

arm. Hasta leads us to the right in the next hallway. We are surrounded by white tubing. "You have always been popular with certain people. Certain people with power."

"Jaigon wants to know, just like you did, how I found you. And the answer will not be what he wants to hear."

Mon pretends to pass out and falls against the wall. "The drama. Whatever will you do?"

"Answer the questions that I am asked, then leave."

Mon grunts as another group of middle held Auraless pass us in the hallway. They stop talking when they notice me. We flatten ourselves against the wall. Different rooms extend out from either side of the hall. They are cavernous. The corners are all square. The Paix only builds with round, finished edges. "Definitely built before the Paix. It extends beyond the stone circle."

"Umm-humm."

I continue to dissect our surroundings. I hate everything about Under Stone. Besides the hard edges, the Under Stone is clinical. Things were built to be plain and functional. Huge bunches of wires snake across the walls in clumps. Metal grates are over holes in the wall and beneath our feet. Our footsteps sound shallow. The air is stale. "This looks like a fallout shelter from the Fusion Wars."

"It does not."

Jaigon overheard my comment. Hasta almost runs into him. Hasta grabs Mon's arm, and they continue down the hall, leaving me alone with Jaigon. "It was made by the Tunnel people. Similar purpose, but never used. No one was able to reach it from the city before every Being was eliminated."

"But the Tunnel people did not inhabit the inner West. So how do you know it was never utilized?"

"What was the inner West became the West coast after the Earthquakes."

I Feel Jaigon's frustration, and then concern. I do not want to argue. "I see."

"Stop doing that," Jaigon says and takes a step toward me.

"What?"

"You stare at me like that, and there is nothing behind your eyes. Then you are like them."

I can think of nothing to say, so I touch Jaigon's hand.

He takes my hand in his and examines it. Eventually, he looks into my eyes. "We did not leave you."

"I know," I say and squeeze his hand. He looks at me as he did when I was a younger held. Warmth creeps into my being. Jaigon's eyes move to my mouth, and I sway forward.

Jaigon drops my hand abruptly. "I found this after one of your circle connection attempts purely by chance. Since you are connecting..."

"Not connecting. Drifting. Serving as a receptacle for unknown entities."

Jaigon raises his eyebrows and puts his hands behind his back. The material of the Under Stone darker clothes accentuates his form. He looks taller and purposeful. "I am sorry. Since you were reporting so much progress with Drifting in the Paix, I could not tell you of my growing concerns. You grow closer to them now."

"I do not," I say defensively. "These voices connect to me. Forcefully."

"I can no longer treat you the same. You are at the fringes of the Paix, and I fear for our existence as Auraless."

"But I am Auraless."

"I fear that you will choose the Paix over us. Not willingly, but as part of the collective mind."

I am hurt by Jaigon's words. "Then stop ordering me to Drift."

"I cannot. Our people must..."

"Survive," I say before Jaigon does. "You are telling me that I may be a casualty."

I Feel Jaigon's emotions sway, but only for a moment. Jaigon assumes his Leadership voice. "Gather information in your Drifting. I will call the others with your Talent to the meeting room. Report your findings to me, especially any connection."

His words sting. "I do not connect. I have no Aura. Not a whole one, not a half. None of us do."

Jaigon's eyes are filled with sadness. "You found us quickly." He walks away.

I am left alone in an unfamiliar, unfriendly tunnel. I wish now that Mon had stayed with me. No one is around to answer my questions or direct me to the meeting room. "I do not know where to go."

Disconnect. Leave. Depart.

"Why?"

I do not receive an answer.

"Time to walk," I say loudly. I always end up where I am supposed to be. I move to the nearest connecting hallway and explore it. Black and gray cables are everywhere, and a hum radiates from the walls. Silver tubes crisscross the ceiling. Though the Under Stone is not lit or maintained in any way that I understand, I am interested in its functioning design, so I make note of the different-sized conduits. I can ask for information later.

"How could they hope to live in such darkness?"

After several hallways, I get a feel for the floor plan and realize it is truly not that different from the Koja: a main heart with arteries running from the center. The wires and cables connect everything like our Lexicon does.

"The Lexicon."

I step through a low, square opening into another hallway. I have no idea how to find anyone or get anywhere without the Lexicon. My reliance on constant access to its resources is eerily similar to the Paix.

"I am glad that you found us."

Suela is standing in a doorway to my left. A dark purple tunic is pulled tightly across her swollen midsection. Her face is shaped like a moon, and her hair is short, white blonde.

"So am I."

Suela caresses her stomach. "No maternity clothes here."

"You look lovely." I indicate the recessed lighting. "How does this all work? It is a puzzle I cannot solve."

Suela smiles at me and touches her stomach. "Shall I introduce you?"

I am embarrassed and dip my head. The Paix—and by extension the Auraless—greet the unborn. Paix parents communicate freely with their unborn in the womb. "I give an apology." I hold two fingers to my lips—the Paix posture for sorrow. "We have never had an unborn in our midst. How is your newer Being?"

Suela extends her right hand toward me, and I relax. "We are well. Thank you. Your questions are valid and similar to what I asked. Without a Lexicon, it does not seem possible. Hasta and Jaigon have been working on this project for some time."

There is something off about Suela's feelings that make me step closer to her. I Feel disappointment. Each area of Auraless expertise—Mechanical, Kitalu, Leadership, Feelers, History—is led by the eldest. As eldest, Suela was passed over by her own department. "I am sorry. They did not tell you."

"I do not mind, truly. With this new Being in growth, I would not have been helpful. I have been dwelling on its Being. I have many concerns. I wanted to ask if you could tell if the Being is comfortable. If there is an Aura."

I understand her concern. A Being from our kind could have an Aura, and if it did, the child could be taken from her by the Paix. "I can try. May I?"

Suela opens her hands in approval, and I place my left hand on her stomach. I let my mind Drift around the larger mass of Suela's Being and Feel threads of a different Being. The Being is intensely curious, but on the edge of my ability to comprehend.

A sharp consciousness jabs into mine. I flinch but do not stop Drifting. I Feel pleasure, then curiosity. Neither emotion is very intense. I watch a series of images—an eye in an ocean, a rainbow, disconnected shapes. There is no weight behind the images, no thoughts. A delightful laugh fills my mind.

I drop my hand and look at Suela. "There is an eye in an ocean. Peace. A feeling of gentle grace. Laughter."

Suela beams at me and then touches my hand. "Is it ... is there ..."

"I do not know how to tell if there is an Aura or not." I consider the jabbing sensation. "But it is a strong Being. It connected to me in thought with threads similar to the Paix. Different, but familiar."

Suela's face loses color. "I was hoping ... I do not want to ... it is my child."

I Feel Suela's suffering. Her worry is palpable. "I really cannot ..."

Suela stops me. She takes a deep breath and puts her hands on her stomach. "I understand. It is like these cables. They connect to a grid powered by solar energy. You have your own cables. Your switches work only in the way that they are built to work."

"Exactly. I cannot change who I am or how I work, even when I want to."

"None of us can. I hope this Being will not have an Aura. I would not give the child to the Paix."

"Perhaps you would not have to."

Suela searches my face. "I would not. Partings." She raises her hand to me, then steps into the room and shuts the door behind her.

"Partings," I reply. I Feel Suela's concern deeply. I would not be able to part with my own child, either. Sighing, I continue down the hallway. I let my mind Drift. I turn right and collide with a body.

"Lisle," Joo-roo says awkwardly and holds my arm. He almost loses his balance but rights himself.

"Joo-roo."

"It was my will to stay with you until you awoke, but Jaigon ordered us to evacuate."

"I know."

Joo-roo offers me his arm. I take it. "Where are you going?"

"I do not know my destination," I say and continue with him down the corridor. "I am to meet with those of my kind. Jaigon did not tell me where the meeting rooms were."

"I know where they are. I will show you."

"Thank you."

"What does that mean, your kind?" Joo-roo asks.

"According to Jaigon, my kind is different from your kind." Several Auraless ten helds flow around us. One of them touches my arm and scurries away. "As my Talent grows, the line separating me from the Paix is thinner. Jaigon is concerned that I may break through and become Paix. Risk the Auraless."

Joo-roo opens the door at the end of the hall for me. It is metal like the walls and heavy. The handle is a turning wheel. "He is behaving like an Emperor."

I walk through the door and am surprised to find a large meeting space. The ceilings are high, and several long, silver tables with matching metal benches fill the room. Beazle and Tamar are sitting quietly at a center table. Their hands are folded together. "Our continuance may be at stake. He is being careful."

"Emperor. They wait for you. We do not serve a collective. Remember, we have choice."

"Yes. Joo-roo . . ."

Joo-roo waits. I choose my Words carefully. "There has been a strange . . . duality . . . in your emotions. Are you well?"

"I struggle," Joo-roo says simply. He puts his hand on my shoulder and leaves. He closes the door carefully behind him. His Words trouble me.

"Drift. Focus."

"Beazle, Tamar." I join them at the center table but sit across from them. The metal is cold and unyielding beneath me. I Feel their apprehension. "Where are the others who can Feel as we do?"

"I do not know." Beazle reaches his hand out to me, and I take it. "They told us to come in here. I do not know why."

"Who is they?"

"Jaigon and Hasta," Tamar replies in a small voice. "Do you know why?"

"Because we are important. We must focus together and understand the reason our Yuan is failing and the Paix is sick. But we need Rebekah and Shanthi. The others are not ready, and Zaron is too young."

"We are not like them now, are we? I do not want to be like them."

Beazle's voice is filled with hatred. I Feel that he is angry with himself. "Explain your words, Beazle."

"I am frightened. They think we are more like the Paix. I am not. I am Auraless."

"They know that," I reply evenly. "Jaigon needs us to use our Talent."

"I will not cooperate," Beazle says in a grownup voice. He runs to the door and screams when it does not open. I do not stop him. His warring emotions must be voiced to bring calm to his Being.

Shanthi enters the room. She is only two spance my junior. Her hair is black and almost past the tips of her fingers. She is so beautiful, she seems to glow. Her teeth are white and straight, and the darkness of her clothing blends into the tone of her skin. If I squint, I cannot tell where one begins and the other ends. We are not social friends, but we do compare our experiences in the development of our Auras. She also tests once a week.

Shanthi puts her hand over Beazle's heart, and he stops screaming. She strokes his hair, then brings her fingertips together several times. He catches his breath. Shanthi leads Beazle back to the table. "Rebekah cannot Feel. I have excused her from our meeting."

Rebekah is only six held, and I consider that perhaps her mind has shut down to protect her. "It is for the best."

Shanthi sits by me, and Beazle edges close to her. Tamar keeps her distance from Beazle but holds the edge of my sleeve. Shanthi folds her hands. "We are gathered. We wait for your instructions as eldest held."

I Feel Shanthi's calmness, and it quiets my mind. "Thank

you. Jaigon has asked our group to Drift. What is happening to the Paix? Why are their systems failing? We must see if we can gain information for the Auraless to help them."

"Will they eliminate us?" Beazle asks.

Tamar pulls on my sleeve, and I put my arm around her. "No."

Shanthi clucks her tongue. "We may have a Talent that separates us, but we are with our kind. I Feel this truth. We must attempt this for the Auraless. They count on us."

Beazle and Tamar nod, and Shanthi takes a deep breath. I close my eyes. "Drift. Listen and learn."

My thoughts Drift from the meeting room. I see myself as a small dot at a long table. I cannot find the strings to the collective Paix, so I call for my Father mentally.

"Father. Please. What is happening?"

My vision blurs, then narrows. I am a child, helpless in a clear crib. I want to be picked up, and I hold my arms up. My parents watch over me, motionless. They cannot connect to me. My Father is made from metal, and my mother from bones except for her lips, which are flesh. Red rims them.

My Father looks away from me, and I am airborne. There are multi-colored balloons tied to my grown Being. I float over my Strand and Tether. The homes are empty, and the Paix are gone. I am light. Large butterfly wings flap on the ground next to my shadow. There is no body attached to the wings. The balloons pop, and I fall, but the ground moves away from me.

There is no ground.

CHAPTER 7

Many spances passed in equanimity. Then the first earthquake came, and with it, cracks in the Tunnel Cities. The Infrastructure itself was damaged, but the real cracks were between the peoples. Distrust festered between the people of the Nations under the Leadership and the Indigo Children. The Indigo Children were evolving. The next generation of Indigo Children formed Auras. The Others in the Leadership did not understand the new genetic abnormality.

—HISTORIES OF PAIX, INDIGO 3.15

I OPEN MY EYES. BEAZLE and Tamar are watching me. "Use your Words."

"There are no more strings," Beazle says triumphantly. "You told me to look for them, and I have seen them before, but not anymore."

I Feel great relief within Beazle. Tamar nods in agreement. They smile at each other. "It is like we are normal."

"We are normal." Shanthi's eyes are still closed. "We wait for Shanthi."

When she finally opens her eyes, I Feel sadness in her Being.

"The strings are shorn," Shanthi says in a shaky voice. "There is one with scissors, and balloons, multi-colored balloons . . ."

"I saw the balloons," I confirm. "They popped. I fell, but never hit the ground. Nothing was real. I also saw . . ."

Jaigon bursts through the door to the meeting room and walks to our table. Beazle hides behind Shanthi. Tamar does not move, but she does grasp my hand under the table. She begins to cry.

"Why do you run, Beazle?" Jaigon asks.

Beazle shakes his head vehemently.

Jaigon sits down at the table next to me and touches my knee. He taps on it three times, then lets it linger. I do not know if this motion is an apology to me or confirmation that I am really present. I do not care, as it makes me happy.

Jaigon lifts his hand. "Why is this child crying?"

Neither Beazle nor Tamar answer Jaigon. "They are frightened," I whisper. "Use their names."

Jaigon softens his voice. "Tamar, Beazle. I rediscovered this Under Stone for our protection. You are both safe here. We all are."

Tamar and Beazle nod timidly. Jaigon indicates the seat next to him. "Beazle, sit."

Beazle does not comply.

"He is afraid that you will eliminate him," I blurt out. "Us. For Feeling."

Jaigon looks at me with incredulity.

"We are different. You have said as much to me."

Jaigon addresses Beazle. "We do not eliminate our own. Have not this fear. I am your Leadership. I protect you."

Beazle finally sits next to Tamar. I Feel his tension recede. "Perhaps Beazle and Tamar can leave?"

Jaigon nods consent.

The children dart out of the meeting room. I wait until the door closes, then turn to Jaigon. "There are no threads for the younger ones. Rebekah has no sense of weight at all. She was excused from this meeting."

"What does that mean? Threads, weight?"

"They do not sense the Paix's presence at all," I respond.

"The collective is not operating as normal," Shanthi says at the same time.

"How do you both know this?" Jaigon asks.

"I Feel it," I answer simply. "Waves of desperation. Balloons made of colors that cannot be held, only tied. Their way of life is disrupted."

"I Feel it as well," Shanthi confirms. "It was as if our Feeling was in color. The younger helds are not as skilled and could Feel nothing. The Paix cannot function like this. It is unnatural."

Disconnect. Depart. Leave.

A thought grips my mind. "But what if the Ortus can? If it is programmed to find help?"

Shanthi holds her hand out to me. "Yes. The Paix are crippled and relying on their combined mind in the Ortus to function for them."

The room begins to buzz. My body jerks, and I Feel Words in my Being that are not my own. My mouth moves.

"The Ortus cannot function correctly with a Singularity. System Failure."

Jaigon brushes his fingers against my cheek, then rests his hand on my shoulder. "Come back to us, Lisle."

I look at Jaigon in surprise. "I have not gone anywhere."

"You were glowing. An Aura . . ."

"Glowing is not an Aura."

Jaigon stands and lets his hand fall down my shoulder. He takes a strand of my hair between his fingers and studies it. "Silver. That is what the glow is."

"There is no silver Aura," Shanthi says. "It is not on the wheel. But . . . your voice was different. What do you mean about the Ortus?"

I try to pinpoint where the Words have come from, but I cannot. I do not want to tell Jaigon this. Shanthi knows. "The Ortus is dependent on the Paix as we are. It will fail when they do. It needs us to correct the system failure."

"Which is the Singularity? The virus?"

"Yes. That is the simplest way to understand it. Shanthi?"

"I agree."

Satisfied, Jaigon leaves. "I will share this information with the Chai. For now, you may wish to explore the Under Stone."

Disconnect. Depart. Leave.

The sharpness of the voice in my mind frightens me.

"Why? Who are you?"

I need to tell Jaigon about the voices. "Jaigon?"

Shanthi pulls her hair over her shoulder. It trails the table top. "He is gone. He has the Deepness for you. I Feel it even now."

I dismiss Shanthi's Words. "Jaigon cares for all in this community. It is his duty."

"But for you, there is the Deepness. There is history, trust. Time spent in youth, a longing."

Shanthi's Words are true. "When I was young, we spent much time together. Now, he does not seek my company. It is as if he has forgotten our friendship. He has forgotten me as Lilse. I am Subject 46."

Shanthi looks at me strangely. "And you feel Deepness for him. This is . . ."

"Not your concern," I say abruptly and stand. "I understand why our presence makes some Auraless feel uncomfortable. Do not read my emotions, Shanthi."

"I will not share these Words with others. You are open to me now. You rarely are."

"I do not mean to be."

"And yet you are," Shanthi says musingly. She purses her lips. "I will leave this topic for a more pressing one. There are two voices in your mind. Possibly three."

I sink back into the bench. "They connect to me."

Shanthi studies me. "We cannot know what part they play. We must awaken the Paix. They sleep."

"I Felt more of a waiting, as if an event is expected."

Shanthi raises her delicate eyebrows. "An event?"

"Like a decision must be made for the Paix. There is a question unanswered, and this is the virus. The butterfly, the balloons—these are foreign images. Singularity."

"The question must be answered," Shanthi whispers.

"Yes. By us. We are the only ones who can hear the question."

Shanthi tilts her head to the right and regards me. "You and I must go to Paix. I have a family there as well. An Auraed little brother."

Standing, I take Shanthi's hand in mine. "With or without Jaigon's approval."

Slivers of metal are sewn into Shanthi's skirt, and they jingle happily when she stands. "Agreed. We wait for the decision of the Chai, then act accordingly."

I place my left fingertips on top of Shanthi's collarbone. She reciprocates. The pact is made in Paix Ritual.

"I will show you to your quarters," Shanthi says. "Or at least where I think they are. The schematics were shown at Assembly, but I do not digest diagrams well."

I laugh, as Shanthi's phrasing is interesting. "We do not eat Words."

"That is my conversation."

"It is good," I say and follow Shanthi from the room. The hallway is dim, but lit enough for walking. After several twists and turns, we come to a wing that branches off to the left. We enter a round waiting area that looks like the stone circle above us. Feisel, an older held Electrical, has an array of Lexicon and Replicator pieces set up in the middle of the floor.

I catch my breath. Everything is identical to the circle above us except the smell. Instead of fresh and forest-y, the air is damp and musty. I drop to my knees right through the image of a large stone. The floor is metal like the walls. I touch it, and my hand passes through tufts of wet grass. "What is this?"

"Optical illusion," Feisel explains. His shirt is smeared with dust, and his angular face shines with sweat. His dark eyes dart around the room intelligently. "The stones serve as viewing extensions. Thin wires with reflective glass in them snake to the surface and thread through the stones. They produce this reflection for us."

"But . . ."

"Easily done with mirrors," Feisel says. "Ingenious for the era. This is a real-time representation of what is on the surface. The only connection to the above world, besides rain water feeding the collection troughs, of course. And the venting system. Compressed air, quite advanced."

"Of course," I echo. I rock back on my heels and look at the ceiling. It is cloud-covered, and lightening snakes across it. "What does that mean?"

"Those who built this sanctuary prepared it for long term use. Basic needs handled in a sophisticated fashion, for the time. Even the waste is used for energy supply."

I crawl forward and pass through another stone. "All of the stones serve this function?"

"Yes. There are nineteen of these rooms near each living area."

Shanthi walks through a tree. "It is an illusion I would not wish to see if I were trapped down here."

"But they also carry sound," Feisel says. He moves a long, cylindrical piece of equipment. "Much like our Paix ancestry, they would want to keep tabs on the surface. I would not wish to live underground permanently."

I reach the wall and touch it. It is cold and rough. "No one ever did."

"That is where Jaigon is wrong," Feisel responds. "The Histories, too. I believe at least one person did. This place was shut down meticulously from the inside."

Shanthi's robes swirl as she turns to face Feisel. "A journal? Evidence?"

Feisel looks shocked. "How do you know that? Can you Feel through . . ."

Shanthi laughs. "I do not Feel the dead, do not worry. I Feel you. You are intrigued by the mystery."

Feisel runs his hand through his hair. It is long and unruly. "Yes, I am. Sorry. I found a video journal. He was accompanied by a canine. He was deaf and did not speak, so the Listeners did not find him. It is pictorial, and the language is by hand. I have asked permission to decipher it, but Jaigon wants all of these systems checked out first. He thinks it is from before the Wars. I differ."

"Prudent," I say. I Feel Feisel's displeasure. "He acts as Leadership. Keep us safe, then find your answers."

Shanthi touches her forehead to her heart, which is the Paix symbol for truth. "You will find the truth and correct the History. Let us leave this false place, Lilse. It is for broken dreams."

I hurry through the room, but take one last look at the sky. "I hope he did not live here alone long."

"Why?" Feisel asks.

"We need each other. It is hard to be alone."

Feisel holds up a thin cable in his hand. "For some."

I smile. Feisel is different. That is what is wonderful about being a Feeler. I never know what kind of emotion I will pick up. It is always different, as each Auraless is unique. "Partings."

Feisel lifts his hand. He does not look up from his project. **Disconnect. Leave. Depart.**

I hurry to catch up to Shanthi. The hallway connects to another large, round space. Several Auraless are gathered. Shanthi is speaking to Mithras, one of our Kitalu workers. There are interesting designs on the wall, colorful furniture, and shapes that are missing from knee-tall tables. Animal caricatures imprint the floor. I recognize some from the Safari.

Several square receptacles are recessed in the floor. Zaron is playing in one of the receptacles. He notices me. I smile at him. He claps and returns to his play. I join Mithras and Shanthi. "The Kitalu?"

"It would seem so," Shanthi responds. "Each living area has

one."

"They hoped for a future." The furniture is stark, but inviting—made for children and their parents. Several swings and other playthings are tucked into alcoves. "And all still functioning."

"Jaigon worked to restore this one only," Mithras said. "The other Kitalu areas are not functioning."

"Jaigon is thoughtful for his people."

"If only we had more play objects," Mithras says.

I smile. Jaigon would forget those—like our hair combs.

"Perhaps we can fashion some," Shanthi says. "I will assist you in this. Partings."

I mirror Shanthi's gestures to Mithras and follow her through the Kitalu. I Feel a sense of contentment, true joy from the youngest helds, and it makes me hopeful. "The children have adjusted. Perhaps we can as well."

"It has been only hours," Shanthi says. "Soon, they will miss the Earth above." She puts her hand over crude numbers etched into the metal of the nearest doorframe. "We are meant to live in the light."

I Feel Shanthi's unhappiness. "It will not be for long."

Shanthi closes her eyes. "I hope not. Down this hall is the number block for your quarters. The hallways radiate out like the arms of our Tethers and Strands, Salles and Calles. Compare it to the Koja—it will help you orientate."

The similarity is strangely comforting and alarming at the same time. "Shanthi . . ."

"I like to think the oxygen became thin for him. It is hard to live in air that has surrounded death so closely."

I think of the sole survivor. Alone, without family. I Feel my own sorrow for such an end. Shanthi is waiting. I clasp her hands. "Partings."

"Partings."

Shanthi squeezes my hands, then moves gracefully down the hallway. I explore the hallway but do not look at any of the other radiating common rooms. When I come to 46, I open the door by turning the knob and pushing inwards.

At first glance, the room is nondescript and small. There is no decoration. My pack is on the single bed. Everything is brown, gray, or black. There is a chair, a locker, and a sink with a large mirror.

Mirrors of this size are rare in the Koja. They are not part of Paix culture. I peer into the mirror at myself curiously—do I look the same away from the Koja, away from what I have always known?

I trace my nose and cheekbones with my fingers. My face is very symmetrical. I am not displeased with it. My eyebrows are straighter than most. I part my lips, then close them. I intone my vowels and memorize how my teeth and tongue move to make the sounds. My light hair frames pale skin and hazel eyes. The image in the mirror mimics my motions. I smile. Then I frown.

I turn away from the mirror. My face is that of my Mother's, and yet . . .

I sit down on the bed and bend forward. I am queasy, but it passes. Standing, I walk back to the mirror and look in it again. My eyes are paler than I remember them to be. I look more closely, and I am sure that the color has lightened. I hold a piece of my hair between my fingers. It is lighter.

I sit heavily on the bed and take my personal Lexicon from my pack. I hold it, but it does not connect. I take out my Paix Aura shoes and put them underneath the bed.

An Aura.

I hang my pack off the end of the bed and lie down. I imagine my parents' faces, then Feel emptiness.

CHAPTER 8

The Indigo Children welcomed the evolutionary change in their new generation. But when several children were born with yellow eyes, the Others began to question what was happening within the minority of their own Leadership. Fearing for their future, the Indigo Children sent a team of explorers to the surface of the Earth without the auspices of the Others. This team completed toxicity tests, sweeps for Listeners, and basic surveying to determine if the surface was habitable.

—HISTORY OF PAIX, INDIGO 3.18

"THE YUAN CONTINUES to disintegrate," Hasta says in a matter of fact tone. "The Auraless must take action to preserve the atmosphere. Heat is our most pressing concern."

We are at Assembly in the meeting room. There is no working mass communication network in Under Stone, so Jaigon convened us by contacting one representative from every spance, who then gathered those of their spance. Rayel—eldest in my spance—had to knock on my door three times before I woke up.

"Focus."

Some of the conversation has been about how to maintain a food supply without Replicators. The rest has been about the Yuan's continued degradation.

Jaigon sits in a single, black chair in the front of the room. It is square and sparse. "I open the floor."

"The Far has not been investigated in over two hundred spances," Suela says and stands up. She puts her hand on her stomach and continues. "When the Yuan fails completely, we do not know what will infiltrate. I recommend remaining underground."

Jaigon nods. "Thank you for your contribution."

Suela sits down, and another Auraless stands and speaks about the troubling climate situation.

Mon rolls her eyes. "Why do we not just go to Paix now before everything completely fails? We can sort it out."

I do not disagree with Mon's sentiment. "It is imperative that we go. There is no other way. I prefer it to be . . ."

Jaigon's voice cuts through my words. "Subject 46 and Subject 52 have reported that the collective mind is . . ."

Jaigon waits for me to complete the statement. "Operating inefficiently," I supply and seek Shanthi in the crowd. When I find her, I indicate that she should stand and complete our report.

Shanthi stands. "The Ortus speaks for the Paix presently. We will not know what the effects of a broken collective are until a reconnaissance party is sent to Paix." Several of the Auraless murmur, but Shanthi does not change her posture. "Our recommendation is to journey to Paix immediately and seek the Ortus after detailing the Paix condition."

"I do not disagree," Jaigon replies. "The Chai will vote."

Mon leans forward to watch the process. Her entire body is energized. "Just vote already. If I were on the Chai, this would be done, and we would be heading out."

I smile at Mon's Words. I imagine she will run for a place on the Chai next spance and make the governing process more streamlined. If we have another spance.

I Feel Joo-roo's eyes on me. "Not an emperor," I mouth to

him, but he shakes his head and looks away. I Feel indecision and suffering within him.

The Chai call out their answers. There are only two Dissenters. Since the overwhelming majority votes in Affirmation, we all clap three times.

"The Chai is heard by this Assembly," Jaigon says. "The Auraless will answer your call. A reconnaissance team will leave in one hour's time for Paix. Each department will prepare their eldest held Leadership for journeying. We will meet at the main exit."

Suela stands, and Jaigon recognizes her. She puts her hands across her abdomen. "I cannot journey. I appoint Hasta as acting eldest. He has developed this Under Stone with you. You have seen his abilities. He is qualified."

"Agreed, Suela. Hasta?"

"Accepted."

"I will go as well," Sarta says. She walks to the center of the room. "It is my place to journey as Eldest held. I wish to hold my parents' hands again."

Jaigon bows to Sarta. "Acquiescence is granted."

No one else says anything, and Jaigon moves his arms down in a heavy fashion. "Assembly is complete. Rations are available in the Meal area now."

The Auraless spill out of the room. They do not form up by spance or discipline. No one is dressed the same, so visual cohesiveness is lost. It is not quite pandemonium, but the Auraless Feel disorganized.

"Starving," Mon says and hurries away before I can speak to her. I remain seated, as I can Feel that Shanthi wishes to speak with me. I wait and am not surprised when she sits next to me and says, "Shall we both go?"

Disconnect.

The heaviness in my Being is acute. "No. There must be someone left to guide the children's Talent to the threads."

"If you do not return? Do you anticipate . . ."

"I know nothing. We do not see the future, you and I, only

Feel the present. I Feel danger. The children will need guidance. You will serve this purpose admirably."

"Then I wish you success."

"Thank you," I say and bow my head to her.

We both stand and move to opposite exits. My mind is occupied, but I am not alone for long. Joo-roo finds me in the dwindling crowd and falls into step next to me.

"You will go?" Joo-roo inquiries.

"I shall."

"I will not," Joo-roo says. "To Paix, at least. I am not Eldest held of our department."

"I am."

"So, you go. But the Far . . . it calls to me."

I stop walking and look at Joo-roo. He has never liked the collective, but I even Feel more within him now. There is an underlying discontent I do not understand. "The Far?"

Joo-roo inclines his head. I Feel that he is searching for something within himself, but does not find it. "What do you mean about the Far?" I finally ask.

"I wish to see what lies beyond the edges of the Yuan. I wish to . . ."

"Explore?"

"Yes. With Jaigon gone, I have the freedom to leave."

"Is it that way?"

"I do not like being ruled. So yes, it is that way."

I turn into the hallway that leads to my quarters. I Feel discontent within Joo-roo, and though he is my friend and I wish for his safety, I know that he must go to find his own happiness. "I understand."

Joo-roo touches my arm. His fingers are warm against my flesh. He pats my arm, then clears his throat. He says ceremoniously, "I am concerned about this journey. For you."

I stop in front of my door and reach for the scanning pad, then remember it is not there. I grasp the door handle. "As I am concerned for you. You will be alone. Will you reconsider?"

"I will not."

"I knew you would not. Then go knowing that you are held in Deepness by your family."

"And by you?" Joo-roo asks abruptly and grabs my hand. "I will wait for you, if you would go with me."

Surprised, I look more closely at Joo-roo. I Feel within him a Deepness for me that I had not realized was there.

"Come with me."

"Joo-roo, you are my friend, and I hold you to me always. There is a bond between us that I cherish."

"But only a bond," Joo-roo says sadly.

I Feel disappointment, pain—and great anger. There is a war within Joo-roo that I cannot grasp the meaning of. It hurts me. I finally say, "We will Record these journeys separately, and when we meet again, we shall share in our triumphs."

Joo-roo steps away from me. He breathes heavily. He shakes his head several times like he cannot make up his mind. "It will be Recorded, but for whom? Do not trust Jaigon. Do not trust the Paix. Do not trust me. Question everything."

Joo-roo's emotions are chaotic. I force myself to stop Feeling. "It is not for us to trust, but to do. And ask questions."

"I . . ."

Joo-roo's Words fail. I take his hands in mine. "Do not be troubled. You are a true heart. Thank you, Joo-roo." I point to my heart with my index finger and place my hand on his chest. Joo-roo repeats the gesture, then backs away from my room.

"That shall be my last Paix ritual."

"So be it," I say. "It is a meaningful one." Joo-roo turns the corner, and I close the door. I lean against it. I remember the classes that Joo-roo and I shared, the conversations. I Feel the loss of Joo-roo keenly.

Another memory fills my thoughts. I am floating in the sea. I am young and do not remember how I came to be in the sea, just that I am there. Jaigon patiently teaches me how to float. He holds me as if I am precious. I laugh and laugh when water fills my mouth. Jaigon watches me laugh. I Feel his joy through my skin. I tell him so.

That was when he first recognized my Talent. He had seemed proud of me, there in the sea. As I grew, I tried hard to develop and utilize my Talent because of his constant encouragement. If it was so important to Jaigon, then it must be important to me.

"Uggh," I say and throw myself backwards on the bed. If only I could tell Mon . . .

"Mon," I say out loud and sit up. I cannot leave Mon here, Under Stone, while I journey to Paix. I Feel my own panic vividly.

"Mon." I have never been without Mon in my life. We were in Kitalu together, every class. I need to find her. I walk to the door, turn the handle, and push it open.

Mon is standing in front of my door with her palm out-stretched toward the knob. She steps into my room and closes the door. She does not ask how I knew she was outside of my room. "How are we going to get me on this Journey? Because I am going. I have a plan if we cannot think of something above board. I already packed."

Smiling, I embrace Mon. "I am in consideration of this problem as we speak."

"Tell Jaigon you will not go without me," Mon says and sprawls across my bed. "Your gift is the most valuable on this journey."

"That will not work, and you know it. Jaigon can order me to comply as Leadership."

"True. He may Feel competition for your attention. He does not like that. Perchance that is why he truly does not want to go to Paix. I can tell. He does not want to compete with them for you, either."

"That is unfair."

Mon puckers her lips. "Is it?"

I know that Mon realizes that it is unfair. I also notice her flute sticking out of her pack. "The flute! Of course. Music has always been processed by the Paix on a different level of consciousness.

That is your Talent. You must accompany us even though you are not your own department. You are eldest held in this."

Mon looks at her flute, then at me. "To what end? Awaken the Paix? Scare the Paix?"

"Who cares," I say triumphantly. "We can awaken or scare or shock or use whatever term you want. You are the only one who can do any of it. Music is communication without Words. It is valid. Jaigon has to accept your usefulness."

Mon folds her hands beneath her head and looks up at the ceiling. "Some people you journey with even when their reasoning is akin to madness. To the Far, to the ends."

I think of Joo-roo. I feel wetness in the corners of my eyes. "Word."

Mon bounds off the bed. "Then let us go. Let us convince Jaigon of the worthiness of my inclusion."

I grab my pack. I pause and consider it. I never unpacked it. "We will not have to convince anyone of the obvious."

Mon is already halfway down the hallway. I shut my door carefully and put my forehead on it for a moment.

Where are you?

I hurry down the hall after Mon. "We could be gone for a long time. We may never return, Mon. This is serious."

Mon snaps her fingers. "I think it will be a simple solution. One, two, three—wake up. We will be back in the Koja in no time."

Other Auraless press against the wall as Mon and I walk past them. "Why are they looking at us?"

"Because we are journeying, and they are not."

"Well, if you think about it, we all journeyed here."

"In the cold and wet. That alone is something. Auraless are tough."

Another group passes by us, and I avoid eye contact. "But the journey is not so far by foot from the Koja to this Under Stone. Our journey to Paix on foot will be long. Uncomfortable, if the Yuan is still malfunctioning."

"I had not considered that. I am not fond of walking."

"I know. Something to consider."

Mon eyes me warily. "Are you trying to talk me into or out of journeying?"

"I . . ." I swallow my Words. I do not want Mon to suffer. Or not return to the Koja, or Under Stone. I try again. "I worry that you will be . . ."

"Stop worrying," Mon says confidently.

We pass Par in the hallway. She waves to us and puts her fingers on her heart. We both reciprocate the action. I Feel her unease. "The Auraless do not think we will return," I say to Mon when we stop in the middle of the next walk through. "I want you to know that not returning is a real possibility."

Mon raises her eyebrows. "Do you?"

A group of younger helds with their Keep Safes move towards us down the hall. I put my pack in front of me, and we pass each other single file. I fiddle with the buckle on my pack. "Do I what?"

Mon pulls the strap of my pack. "Come on. Tell me what you think. Or what you Feel."

"I do think we will return. But only because I cannot imagine not returning. I do not Feel anything."

"There are no certainties," Mon says and pushes me forward.

"But I should be more . . . knowing, or Feeling, or something."

"Why should you be? Who cares if we come back or not if we do not have a Yuan and we cannot grow food stuffs. Or Replicate food stuffs."

"No food stuffs."

"Correct," Mon says. "These are greater concerns. The Mechanical has been working on non-Paix Replicators for some time. The problem is that the molecular content of things we need are not known to us."

"Like food."

"Exactly. That information is transferred to the Replicators by the Ortus, and Mechanical cannot decipher it yet. We are kept like pets."

"Not pets," I argue. "That was forbidden by the first Paix. No slavery."

"There is slavery, and there is slavery."

We both stop, as we have reached the main exit. Hasta is already present, as well as Jaigon and Chur.

"Mon is not a department head," Jaigon comments.

Mon sticks her chin up. She raises her flute and waves it in the air. "I represent my Talent. I am eldest held in music."

"Which is not a department," Chur says. He is the Historian of the Auraless, our Recorder. His task is to visually codify the events that happen to us and pass this information to the Paix via the Lexicon. Each year, he adds to the Lexicon of the Auraless as well. Chur's face is thin, and his lips are fleshy. Many of the younger helds believe him to be very attractive for this reason. His most outstanding feature are his eyes—large, pale, and watchful.

Jaigon studies Mon. "Acceptance. You may be useful. Record this addition."

Mon grabs my hand, and we jump up and down silently. Jaigon motions for us to be still. "We must wait for Sarta and Rastin before departing."

Jaigon turns the wheel of the heavy exit door to the left. Gears grate against each other and the wheel clicks loudly. After several rotations, it no longer turns, and Jaigon pushes the entire wall forward, then to the left. The space behind the wall is narrow and lit with two parallel ceiling light strips. I see a small landing through the aperture, then a series of black mesh steps that lead upwards.

Jaigon addresses us. "Rastin is here. Sarta has five minutes to arrive."

I do not know Rastin well. He is quiet, dark, and brooding, but highly skilled in Electrical functions. I am glad that he is joining us.

Rastin rests his hand on the ground in front of the exit.

"Where does this lead? I need to mentally diagram our location."

Jaigon stands in the exit hallway and points up, then forward. "The Portal's stairs lead to the cave before the Bahn."

The Bahn was the roadway that connected major cities to each other during the Ancient times. Parts of it is still in existence, as the Indentured maintain it.

Hasta hums a nursery rhyme—Over the Hills. I recognize it from Kitalu. The concept of a grandmother always fascinated me. He finishes humming the last few notes and leans against the wall. "So, we have Mechanical, Electrical—whatever you are, Mon—Feeling, History, Leadership, and Sarta."

"I am the eldest held for Music" Mon says. Her face is flushed. "I will, however, answer to Mon. And your pitch is off."

"Perhaps I need a music lesson."

I roll my eyes, but Mon giggles. She proceeds to flirt with Hasta, so I seek out Chur. "Will you record these deeds in Paix format, or just for the Auraless?"

"I can Record events only in our History at present. The Ortus will not currently accept any input from our devices. What is your connection status?"

Chur is always to the point. Since I began developing my Talent, he has asked at every social meeting what my connection status was. My answer has always been more or less the same, but he still asks without fail. "I Drift on the edges, much like the fish of old on the reefs."

Chur takes out his Lexicon. It is Auraless-made and not connected to the Paix. It is not as powerful, nor holds as much knowledge as those of the Paix, but it does serve for our History. "A pity. I will Record your current status. I was hoping that you would be able to connect with your Lexicon via your Talent."

"I cannot," I say with genuine regret. "My apologies."

Chur opens the Auraless Lexicon, types, then shuts it. "We do not have proof that there are no more reefs in the oceans of Earth. Perhaps you should not use this reference to describe your Talent. Sarta has arrived."

Jaigon greets Sarta. I open my hand to Chur. I Feel his aloofness, and it bothers me. "Thank you for your conversation."

"I will Record it," Chur responds evenly. He does not take my hand.

Since I have nothing else to say, I stand by the exit. Sarta speaks with Jaigon. She has a medium-sized pack made of rainbow material in her arms. Rastin is deep in conversation with Hasta. Mon pretends to study her flute, but I know that she is eavesdropping on everyone and every conversation. Chur types.

Where are you? What is this?

The voice is small and confused. So am I.

"What is what? I leave for Paix. Who are you?"

I do not know.

"It is the hour. We depart." Jaigon steps through the exit confidently.

"I must focus."

I follow Chur, and the rest of the group falls in line behind us. We trudge through the shallow corridor extending behind the exit. Lights hang like plant leaves from the walls every five feet.

Chur disappears above me. Ladder rungs are bolted into the metal wall in front of me. I take a deep breath and begin to climb. My hands shake. The rungs are smooth and slick, and my left foot slips. I bang against the wall but keep moving.

When I reach the last rung, I take Jaigon's hand and let him assist me up out of the exit and onto my feet. The first thing I notice is the cold. The second thing I notice is the warmth of Jaigon's hand in mine.

I steady myself and look at Jaigon to offer thanks for his help. For a moment, I Feel the connection we have always had flare inside me. He pulls me roughly to him, and I feel his lips brush against my hair.

"Jaigon, I . . ."

"Shh . . ." He moves his arm around my back. He holds me a moment, and we breath together. "Stay close. We need your Talent."

"But it is . . ."

"I need you." Jaigon kneels beside the exit and helps Mon out.

Warmth floods my body.

"It is like a nightmare," Mon says as soon as she stands. "This is not our world."

I look at our surroundings for the first time. Nothing feels or looks familiar. The rain has washed away our previously marked paths. I recognize the cave front but only see a vague outline of the Bahn—cylindrical curves rising above the earth in the direction of Paix. Many are now broken or cracked.

"The Bahn," I say with deep sadness. The Bahn's intersection with the cave had been a landmark for the Koja since it was established. I would see my parents, then return and know I was nearing the Koja when the large cave next to the Bahn came into sight.

"How could it crumble so quickly? It is from the Ancients," Mon says.

"The Bahn is not of the Ancients," Rastin says and walks between us. "The original construction materials predate them. It is from the Others, possibly even from the Befores. Their history is fragmented because of the Fusion Wars."

Mon rolls her eyes. "Thanks for clearing that up. What are you Recording, Chur?"

"The destruction," Chur says. "Sarta is pointing out things that have changed in the landscape."

"That would be everything."

"Not everything," Hasta corrects. "Just most things."

"We begin the journey," Jaigon says. "Stay close together. I will lead. Rastin and Hasta, protect the rear."

"From what?" Mon asks. "Roving bands of disconnected Paix?"

Jaigon does not answer her. I Feel relief, as at least we are moving. The cold is pressing, and I slow down to dig in my pack for my hand coverings. No one else seems to be affected, but my fingers are already stiff. My face is cold, but I have nothing to put on it.

"Cold?" Sarta asks me.

"Yes. Very. Perhaps because I am a Feeler, the cold affects me more."

"Perhaps. Keep up with the group. We do not know what is out here."

Sarta moves ahead of me. I push my pack behind me and follow her. The trees do not look as welcoming as they seem when I am in the Go-Go. There are clouds in the sky, though the Helio has not yet risen. Without the Bahn lights, semi-darkness grips the Earth. I shiver and run a few steps.

"It will be a little warmer when the Helio rises," Rastin says from behind me. "Not much, though."

"I wish it would rise now." I think about Joo-roo, alone, walking to the Far. "What do you think is in the Far?"

"Nothing," Rastin answers. "The Yuan protects us from the failing atmosphere. Outside it is wasteland. Lifeless. It is why the Brown Auraed chose species to care for and created the Safari."

I visited the Safari once with others of my spance. Many animals roam in this wilderness protected by the Yuan—birds, fish, mammals. Some are friendly, some not.

"You must slow your pace," Chur says. "I cannot Record, and these first minutes are precious to establish the history."

Jaigon slows the pace. The cold changes. The normalized temperature that I have become accustomed to returns. I take my hand coverings off and stretch my fingers.

Jaigon stops abruptly and raises his hand with a closed fist. We stop. I cannot see anything at first, but when I do, I wish I had not. Evidence of mass violence litters the Bahn. Several burned Go-Gos are piled in the middle of the intersection. The Bahn barriers are broken, and part of the roadway is scorched.

I gag and put my hand over my mouth.

Chur Records. "Charred bones, destroyed roadway. The Ritual will have to be done quickly. If at all."

Mon stands next to me and puts her arm around my shoulders. We walk in a circle around the wreckage. I count seven Go-Gos. "They are all from Blue. None are our parents."

One Go-Go's image array is still functioning. Rastin examines it. "They were attempting to aid us. Direct course for the Koja."

"Or eliminate us," Hasta says and pulls a solar panel from the wreckage.

"Aid us," I say firmly.

Jaigon investigates the wreckage with great care. "These two collided on purpose. I am not sure if the others did or not."

"Which indicates that the Paix is eliminating itself?" Rastin asks. He powers down the image array. "It was not machine failure. This was induced by loss of directional thought control of the pilot. Or the Ortus."

"Are they not both machines?" Chur asks and continues to capture footage.

"They are not," I say abruptly and turn from the wreckage. "The living Paix power the Ortus."

"It is definition dependent," Rastin says mildly. "Regardless, they are Ceased."

System failure.

I drop to my knees and touch the ground. It is wet. I Feel a sense of despair, a need for rest. "We must care for their remains."

Jaigon picks up a cylindrical gear, then drops it. "We cannot bring them to the cliffs. They are not our kind. And we cannot carry them to the Ortus."

"No," I say and walk off the Bahn. "But they must be attended to. We will burn them, as they did of old. Like the Ancients. It will suffice. There must be dry . . . oh, they have already been burned. And there is no one to perform the Ritual."

"Stop," Jaigon says and grabs my arm. He holds me still for a moment and traces the shape of my eyebrows with his fingertips. "So beautiful."

I wait. The moment passes. "They must be attended to."

Jaigon sighs. "It shall be done. Let the others gather the dry materials. Sarta will direct them. She cares for the Ritual, too. I need you to . . ."

"I know. Drift. Feel why this happened." I close my eyes and Drift. I Feel nothing. There is an emptiness that surprises me, as before there was need for rest, for Finalities. There are no threads. "It is quiet. Empty. Calm."

Jaigon takes my hand in his. "That is good. Come, let us gather for the Ritual."

He leads me back to the Bahn. Mon joins us and walks beside me. Sarta and Chur wait for us at the edge of the wreckage. Their arms are filled with branches of varying shapes and sizes. Sarta and Chur place the kindling in the center of the crash.

"It is ready," Sarta says.

Rastin and Hasta have created an electric loop from the Go-Gos' wiring. When Jaigon gives the signal, they create a spark. The branches catch fire.

"Say the Ritual," Jaigon directs me.

"There are no Words. It is thought, and only for the Paix."

"You can find them," Sarta says encouragingly and closes her eyes. She opens her hands by her sides, palms to the sky. "Search. We will wait in the posture of respect."

"Drift," Jaigon whispers. He and the rest of the group close their eyes and raise their hands.

I open my mind. I focus on the scene in front of me, the pain, the Ceasing—and fix the image in my mind. I search for the deeper tendril of consciousness I hope must be near.

"Please."

I think this one word as strongly as I can and Drift.

"These are in ending, Ritual . . . these are in ending . . . Ritual . . . Paix . . . these are in ending . . . we cannot return them to the Ortus . . ."

Something sharp cuts through my image. Other eyes are watching through my own. I gasp. My sense of self begins to fight against the invasion of other Beings.

Words tumble from my mouth, then stop. A sense of loss registers in my Being. It is cold, and I Drift in a numbed world. Colorless.

"I will never be one of them."

Words tumble through me until I am in blackness.

CHAPTER 9

The Indigo team found that the Earth's surface was wild, but habitable. Much of the western edge of the continent had fallen away. Few animals had survived the Fusion Wars, but water was abundant. The expedition's conclusions gave hope for a new future. The Leadership imprisoned many Indigo Children when they informed them of their plans to leave. Through the power of the collective mind, most escaped. They left the speakers in the Tunnels and moved West to claim the high Cliffs by the sea for their new, silent race.

—HISTORIES OF PAIX, INDIGO 3.4

"IT IS RECORDED."

Everyone is looking at me. Smoke billows in my face, and I cough. "What is Recorded?"

Chur opens his mouth, then shuts it. He shakes his head at me and looks back at the Lexicon. "Your Words were . . ."

"The first connecting," Jaigon replies in an awed, shaky whisper.

The sound of Jaigon's voice surprises me. For the first time, he sounds unsure of himself. "Connecting?"

Jaigon nods. "You do not remember any of it?"

"I have no recollection of what happened. Are you sure I connected? I do not feel different. I do not have an Aura."

"Oh, yes," Mon says. "The Ritual happened. You spoke strange Words, then mumbled that you would never be one of them. Several times."

"It was more of a chant," Chur corrects, then puts his Lexicon away. "It is Recorded, and the Ritual is complete. The first spoken Word Ritual . . ."

"Ever," Sarta supplies.

"Fascinating," Rastin says at the same time. "Very interesting Word constructions. I will analyze this information at a later time."

"Yes, later," Jaigon says. "Were you in the Paix?"

"No," I respond, but I doubt my own memory.

Jaigon takes a deep breath. "The Words, your gestures . . . they were of Paix. Or perhaps some other language we are unfamiliar with in the Auraless. Something from the Ancients? The Others? Do you remember where the Words came from?"

"I remember a sharp pain and my Being slipping away from me. Then . . ." I jump in recollection. "No—it was taken from me. My Being was taken from me. Eyes that were not my eyes saw through my eyes. Millions of eyes, like all the eyes that ever connected were here, in my mind, and . . ."

I stop speaking, frustrated by the confusion in my own explanation. "They wanted rest. They needed release."

"It was beautiful," Sarta says quietly. "Wherever it came from."

"Take your time," Jaigon encourages. "Continue processing."

And then I know. "The Paix entered me. I cannot connect to them without an Aura, but the Paix can connect to me through their Ceased."

"That is progress," Mon says and puts her arm around me.

"Is it?"

"I think it is."

"Definite progress," Rastin says thoughtfully. "Connecting through their implants, perhaps? A substitute for the missing Ortus?"

Rastin's praise makes me feel better, as he does not give it often. However, tears well in my eyes. My sense of Being is too strong. I can never be a part of . . .

I clap my hands together. "Sense of Being—a Singularity. That is what happened to Subject 6. He could not be in either group."

Jaigon winces at the reference to his friend. Subject 6 had developed an Aura. He connected several times but had jumped from the Koja roof after the last experience. "He chose his own fate."

"But you could be in both," Mon says.

I look at the fire blazing before us. "I do not think so. The weight of the eyes . . . is not for me. There is no Singularity within the Paix."

Sarta steps closer to the fire. "I would like to feel that weight."

Sarta's words trouble me. I Feel her loneliness, her want to belong. "No, you would not."

Sarta starts to say something else, but Rastin speaks over her. "The important question is why did they destroy each other? Did you Feel malevolence or fear? Hatred?"

"No. Loss. Not sorrow. Like discovering that something you had once will never be in your possession again—and then forgetting it immediately."

The rest of the group grows silent, so I walk away from the fire down the Bahn. I plan to continue the journey. Light rain begins to fall, and I wonder if it is the Paix's response to the fire or the Yuan continuing to fail. Or if the Ortus is functioning on its own, trying to save the Paix from the Singularity it cannot contain.

I know that Chur has followed me before I hear his voice. "I understand."

I slow my pace, and Chur walks alongside of me. I Feel his

sorrow, and—empathy. "I do not believe you can."

"I do not think you are different from any of us. We Feel through different mediums."

"What do you mean?"

"I Feel through history and the knowledge it provides me. I have studied the Paix and the collective my entire life."

I look at Chur in a new light. His face is sad and pale in the darkness. He cares for the Paix. "Are you like me, grasping for something you cannot hold?"

Chur smiles ruefully. "Yes. It is as if I am on the edge of a wall, yet I can see the Paix around it and through it, molecule by molecule. They are the family I have Recorded from afar."

I am moved. "Thank you for sharing these Feelings with me. So, I will ask you—what if we do not solve the problem? Will this Earth die?"

"Yes. All things do, except history. What is Recorded remains."

A strange light glows directly ahead on the Bahn. We slow our steps in response to the unknown before us. "Even if there is no person left to read it?"

"It would still be there," Chur replies. "We learned to understand the Ancients through their Recorded Words, their structures."

"The Indigo Children saved them for a reason. The Paix cherishes the wisdom of the old cultures."

"They should have learned from them and rediscovered speech. Even as the Before's structures crumbled, their Words did not. Their Record is still in existence."

"This upsets you?"

"Yes," Chur says. "It is the greatest failure of the Paix to have lost their Words. No one will remember them but us. That is their reality."

"That is a sad thought." The light continues to move in our direction. I think of my Father's Words. "But the Ortus will remember. It holds all their collective thought."

Chur laughs derisively. "There is none that can decipher it. Useless."

Rastin and Jaigon run by us. Mon and Hasta stop beside us and match our pace. Sarta takes up the rear.

"They are scouting," Mon explains. "We watch from a safe distance."

"I should be with them" Hasta says and positions himself in front of Chur. He throws his arms out in frustration. "But I must protect the Recorder and Feeler."

"Do you Feel anything?" Mon asks. "And I can protect myself, Hasta, so stop acting all superior. Sarta, why do you not join us?"

"No," I lie and continue walking. I Feel grief, and I know it emanates from Sarta. It is such a strong feeling, I cannot ignore it. "Sarta follows us. And if Mon can protect herself, Hasta, so can I."

"No doubt," Hasta says. "Yet I was ordered to . . ."

Hasta's voice trails off as the lights come closer. They blink in a pattern. "What are they?"

Rastin and Jaigon have reached the source of the lights. Jaigon yells something I cannot make out. The lights blink several times in unison, then shut off quickly.

Chur runs forward with his Lexicon open. "I am missing it."

Hasta screeches and runs after him. "Jaigon said to wait."

The lights resume blinking. I can barely make out the outline of Jaigon's body and a larger object. As I get closer, I see Rastin holding onto the leg of a floating Go-Go. Chur kneels before it Recording.

Mon yelps in surprise. "Is that a rogue Go-Go?"

Jaigon answers her. "It is. There is no Paix inside controlling it. The navigational system is offline, but we are familiar with it. So, either it was sent for us, sent for them, or it is wandering."

"Sent for us?" Mon asks.

Jaigon waits for Sarta to join the group, then explains. "Perhaps the Paix know our journey's aim from Lisle's Drifting. Or they wish to gather intelligence about their lost."

"More likely, it is wandering," Chur says with conviction. "I cannot Record this properly until the purpose is confirmed."

"Just Record it for now. The reason will become clear."

Hasta smiles. "Record that a means of transport was found floating before us. A gift from the sky."

"It is preferable to walking," Sarta says. "The Earth is crying, and I do not wish to continue on it."

I Feel that Sarta's grief has turned to misery. "We will find your family," I say softly.

Sarta does not pull away from me, but she does look at Jaigon. "We waste much time. Our transportation has arrived."

"Time worth wasting," Chur says and closes the Lexicon. "It is for the future."

"I need assistance to engage this vessel in the present," Rastin says irritably. His hands are dirty, and his shirt is full of mud. "If you are all done worrying about the future."

Jaigon steps around the Go-Go. "Hasta and I will assist you."

Hasta holds the Go-Go's far leg. Jaigon replaces Rastin and holds the Go-Go's front leg. Rastin mumbles something incoherent about hands. Hasta reaches into his pack for several tools and gives them to Rastin.

"Let us give them space," Chur says and walks off the Bahn into a small, natural clearing surrounded by tall trees.

Mon shrugs her shoulders. "Why not join him?"

Disconnect. Depart.

"Stop."

I follow Mon. Chur has found a spacious flat rock, and we share the surface with him. It is smooth and wet. We sit in silence until Mon takes her flute out of her pack.

"I should have played something at the Ritual," Mon says. "There is always music at the Ritual."

"But it is music from the collective thought," Chur responds automatically. "You could not play it correctly—so better to have had none."

Mon ignores Chur and plays. Her music is like a second mind reaching for something it will never attain.

"So beautiful." I lie down on the rock. "Like Words in color."

Rain falls on my face, and I remember my Mother holding my hands and spinning me in the air while I laughed. I was a younger held of five or six. She did not laugh, but I could Feel the laughter of thousands in her body while we spun.

This memory connects to one of Jaigon and the sea. I had pushed away from Jaigon, but I was not ready to swim yet. Water filled my mouth, and I was sinking. I felt the will of thousands pulling me up, pushing me to the surface. Then Jaigon had grasped my waist, and I was safe and coughing.

I could always feel the Paix, though I was never one of them. Until now. I sit up on the rock. I Feel an emptiness around me.

"What is it?" Mon asks.

I shake my head. "Nothing. And everything. The air is empty."

Mon plays a short phrase on her flute. "Well, that is a fascinating thought."

"They have succeeded," Chur interjects. "Perhaps the Journey will move more quickly now."

The Go-Go is functioning. Jaigon beckons to us. "Great," I manage to say. I feel like a moment of great portent has passed and I have not understood it or its value.

Mon replaces the flute in her pack. I Feel her indecision. "It would have been fitting music for the Ritual. Your Talent is worthy."

"Gratitude," Mon replies and winks at me. "Race you."

"Next time. We must be responsible now."

We walk to the Go-Go in silence as a respectable group. It is warmer, and the rain slacks off. Hasta and Jaigon are waiting for us.

"It will be tight in the Go-Go, but we will all fit," Hasta explains. "Mon, you will have to ride in the back flip."

"That is acceptable," Mon says and blinks her eyes several times. I Feel that Mon is thrilled. The back flip of the Go-Go is covered, but not completely. It is used for observing at the Safaris or on trips to gain knowledge about the sky. It is only used at slower speeds.

Mon licks her lips. "It will be quite a ride if we have to break speed protocol."

"You will need to connect via a cable, as we will not maintain average speed," Jaigon explains.

Hasta hands Mon a cable with a hook. She takes it readily and smiles widely. "A dream come true."

The cable makes me nervous. "How do you know that you will be able to control the Go-Go? That is just a cable . . ."

"It is my specialty," Hasta says at the same time Rastin says, "It is a machine."

"Which is or is not connected to an ailing Paix?"

"We will control it," Hasta says confidently and opens the door to the Go-Go. "To be safe, we over-rode the central command processor, and we programmed it to only accept manual input in case it goes back on-line."

Rastin sniffs. "Very rudimentary programming. I did not have much time."

Jaigon pats the Go-Go. "We board and fly."

"I am ready," Mon says. She winks at Jaigon, then follows Rastin and Hasta into the Go-Go.

Jaigon touches my shoulder. "Please board."

"What about Sarta?" I ask.

Jaigon looks toward the tree-line. Sarta is some distance away. Jaigon puts his fingers in his mouth and whistles.

I jump at the sound. So does Sarta. She walks towards us.

"Now will you board?" Jaigon asks.

The rain is becoming steady again, and I do not like the feel of it on my skin. My clothes are damp, and though I know that my spare shirt is dry, I do not want to change in the Go-Go. A glint of light catches my eye, and I notice that the dark is receding to the East of our group. "The Helio rises," I say softly and step into the Go-Go.

"So do we," Jaigon says and watches me climb into the Go-Go.

The Go-Go is dry, and though the space is limited, I feel more secure in its familiar bell shape. Mon has already climbed like a younger held into the back flip. Rastin is at the control console, and Hasta hovers around him, pointing things out on the electrical panels.

I find a space near the back wall. There are several hand holds anchored to it. Sarta's head pops through the floor of the main cabin. She climbs in and stands opposite from me.

I watch Jaigon through the view screen. Rastin manually commands the camera on top of the Go-Go to trace his movements. He walks twice around the Go-Go after we are all inside. He disappears for several minutes, and I wish that the view screen was panoramic.

Jaigon reappears in the front view screen. He ducks down, and I lose him again. He spends a lot of time beneath the front section of the Go-Go, and I wonder if he is checking for potential issues or just clearing his head.

When he finally joins us, he nods to Sarta. Hasta secures the door, and Rastin focuses on working the Go-Go manually.

Jaigon stands behind Rastin. "Activate the shoe holds. Follow the Bahn to Paix. Exceed operational parameters."

I push hard on the raised button on the floor, and a strap secures my right foot. The Go-Go sputters, then turns under Rastin's direction. We glide unevenly, sometimes climbing higher or lower than normal.

Lisle.

I hear my name clearly, and my body stiffens. It is the heaviest voice, full of knowledge and weight.

"Who are you? What are you?"

Depart. Leave. Disconnect.

"We must turn here," I say out loud. "I Feel a presence, and it is ..."

I stop speaking as a wave of nausea overtakes me. A strong feeling of disorientation infiltrates my Being, and then the wall of confusion returns, but it is . . .

"What do you Feel? Which way should we go?" Jaigon asks. "If my senses are attuned, it is to the East. Everything looks different, so confirmation would be useful."

I put my right hand up and touch my thumb to my four fingers. It is the Paix gesture of indication. "I Feel confusion, restlessness, in this direction. This is where we must go. It calls me by name."

"We turn in the direction you indicate."

I gasp and lean over. Jaigon places one arm across my stomach and holds me to him gently. He unlocks my shoe hold and balances my weight between his arms.

Rastin and Hasta bring the Go-Go to a stop, then manage to turn it. Sarta puts her hand on my shoulders.

My insides are twisting. My limbs are like large iron weights attached to my body. A burning sensation runs the length of my throat, and I am lost, lost. I am swimming, but there is no shore. The horizon is slanted, and my stomach churns. Desperation. There is no cohesion to hold me, to hold them, together. "Make it stop."

"They are showing her their pain," Sarta whispers to Jaigon.

Jaigon does not reply. "Hasta, the directions?"

"They do not lead to the center."

"Hold her," Jaigon commands Sarta. I feel the transfer of hands around my waist but remain bent over, unable to straighten.

Hasta shows Jaigon the pathway on the view screen now that the Go-Go has turned. "This is the pathway to the first Tether."

"The Eldest must be the best place to begin. If we cannot discover reason there, then we will move on. Lisle, you must breathe. Breathe as we practiced in the ocean."

I take a series of deep breaths. The nausea fades. I remember when I journeyed with my parents to the first Vociferone. Mother loved to dance beneath the rays of the Helio while Father and I watched. I danced, too, but not like Mother.

Feeling returns to me, and I drop to my knees. Sarta lets me go. I put my hands on the floor to steady myself. Jaigon crouches near me and strokes my lower back in wide circles. The motion is intimate and familiar. "Separate them from you."

Before I can reply, Rastin says, "Jaigon, you need to see this. I think Lisle is Feeling the Indentured."

"That is not possible."

Rastin increases the size on the view screen. A male Indentured comes into focus. He is sweeping an area of land that has been swept clean of grass. It is now a mud pit.

"It has not been told to stop by its program," Hasta says. "That is the only viable explanation for the destruction it is causing."

"But they are individual," Rastin says. "Not pure Machine. He should recognize the damage and know to stop."

"Not with his connection to the Ortus," Hasta says. "He may not be able to update his programming properly now that it is malfunctioning."

"Stop the Go-Go," Sarta says heavily. "Rastin, you can repair this malfunction."

Jaigon looks at Sarta questioningly. "We stop to repair an Indentured? This is not our mission."

Sarta does not look at Jaigon when she speaks. "It will continue to harm the Earth, and preventing that is our mission. He must be cared for. They are not Machines. The programs must be removed, or they will work themselves to death."

<u>System failure.</u>

I hear the third voice and know what we must do. "Please. We must help them."

Jaigon considers, then decides. "I defer to Subject 1 and Lisle, though I do not agree. Stop the Go-Go. Deactivate the Indentured's programs."

Hasta makes a derisive sound. "Let us hope we can start the Go-Go again."

Rastin slows the Go-Go and lands it approximately twenty feet from the Indentured male. "We can if we do not turn her off. Keep the landing gear up and hover, Hasta. I will reprogram."

Rastin slips out of the pilot's console and drops out of the bottom of the Go-Go.

Mon climbs in from the back flip and rests against the inside wall of the Go-Go. "It is getting colder out there."

"We have turned toward the first Tether," Jaigon says. "Perhaps now is when the flute should be played. Music is soothing to the collective mind and, I assume, the Indentured."

"Sure," Mon says and takes it from her pack. "I feel like playing. I feel more like playing than I ever have."

"Not in here" Jaigon says and grimaces. "Out there with the Indentured."

"You can just say you do not like my music."

"I do not like your music. Now go."

"I like your music," I say warmly. "So will they."

Mon smiles. "That is what matters."

Mon plays a haunting scale on the flute, then bends over the exit to climb down. Mon yells when the exit hatch flies open and Rastin climbs into the Go-Go.

"Did you contain the problem already?" Jaigon asks.

"Yes, and no," Rastin says breathlessly. "This male Indentured's program has been deactivated. But look through the view screen. There."

We all gather in front of the view screen. There is a large group of Indentured moving in the Go-Go's direction.

"What are they doing?" Mon asks.

"Searching for answers," Rastin says. "Like us."

Mon snorts. "The difference is, we can communicate. They cannot."

"How do we know that?" Sarta asks quietly. "I am not so sure."

"The Paix cannot communicate with them without their programming from the Ortus," Mon says.

"Neither can we," I say. "We only communicate with them via Lexicon—and the Ortus. We are the same."

"But they cannot communicate at all," Mon says. "We are not

Indentured, nor could we ever be. We communicate with each other. We have Words. They do not. Have you ever heard them speak to each other?"

"Have we ever listened?" Rastin asks. "We have very little contact with them."

Mon opens her mouth to argue, but Sarta cuts her off. "Just play the flute. It will communicate our good intentions to the Indentured."

"And if they do not like what I play?" Mon asks. "They are programmed to do no harm to the Auraless, right?"

"Right," Sarta says.

Mon straightens her shoulders and exits via the ladder without further argument.

I stare down Sarta. "How do you know what they are programmed to do? We really know nothing about them at all."

Sarta looks out of the view screen. "I know."

I Feel Sarta's confidence, so I do not worry about Mon. There is another emotion that I cannot quite fathom within Sarta—regret, but it is mixed with guilt and anger. I wish I could decipher what it is in reference to—but to do that, I would have to have an Aura.

"I will have to deactivate the programs of these as well," Rastin says. "The Paix collective frequency is imprinted in their circuitry."

Jaigon sighs. "They cannot think for themselves?"

"It is not that they cannot think for themselves. They have been programmed not to. For their betterment, according to the Paix."

"For their survival," Sarta says.

Mon's music begins to flow, and it is like water hitting the hull of the Go-Go. Each sound connects to the next, and I Feel a sense of peace fill my mind and Being. I look out the view screen. Something about the Indentured's clothing reminds me of my Mother and Father. Perhaps the Paix fabric or the metal strips that bind the Indentured together. "This is all connected somehow."

"All connected," Sarta repeats. "Bound together by the Ortus. We must care for the Indentured. They are part of us. Jaigon,
I wish this."

Jaigon bows his head. "I defer to the Eldest. Deactivate each
program. Take whatever time is necessary. Hasta, tether the Go-
Go, then help him."

"Thank you," Sarta says.

Sarta and I continue to stare out of the view screen. The Indentured have surrounded Mon, and it does seem as if the music
has a calming affect.

"An interesting choice," Chur says and snaps his Lexicon
closed. "It has been Recorded."

"You have an opinion?" I ask.

Chur looks at Sarta, then me. "I have Recorded. My opinion
is irrelevant, but I repeat—interesting choice."

Jaigon throws a cable out of the hatch to Hasta. "Tie down.
Sarta and Lisle, this is an opportunity for scouting. See what you
can find. Chur, get out and Record. No opinion necessary. I will
remain with the craft."

Sarta exits the Go-Go immediately. Chur follows on her
heels. Although I do not want to leave the warmth of the Go-Go,
I understand why Jaigon wants us to continue searching for directions and vital information. I turn to leave as well, but Jaigon's
hand presses down on my right shoulder.

"Walk with care. Search for anything of value." His lips are
very close to my neck, and I shiver. He pulls me into his arms.
"Do not venture far from the clearing. I no longer trust programming. Go."

The metal rungs of the Go-Go are cold as I climb out into
the open. The air is crisp, and Mon is playing a melody constructed for dancing. I feel the urge to spin, but Sarta is waiting for me
near the Indentured. I join her, and in silence, we walk to the
outer periphery of the clearing. "I Feel the Indentureds' connec-
tions to each other."

Sarta nods.

"Is it really for their own good? The programming?"

Sarta stoops and brushes the Earth with her hand. "Is any of this for our own good?"

Since I cannot answer her, I also stoop and pat the Earth.

"I have never mentioned that a female Indentured would speak to me," Sarta says suddenly. "I was a younger held. There was no one to talk to, but she helped me learn speech. I had forgotten this memory until now."

"How can that be? They do not speak. You began our language, resurrecting it from thousands of years of disuse. The Ortus trained you. I still do not know how you managed to comprehend the letters and the sounds."

"But did I?" Sarta asks.

"Yes, of course," I say in confusion. "It is Recorded in the Ortus. You figured out how to teach the new younger helds as they settled into the Koja."

"That is what the Histories say."

I Feel Sarta's indecision. I offer a solution. "Perhaps an Indentured served as care giver, and you imagined she spoke?"

Sarta is silent for a while, then touches my arm. "Do you believe them to be sentient?"

"Not as we are. They are more like the Paix. Connected by shared work and the Paix mind to the Ortus. Just . . ."

"Cast offs. Like us."

"Yes. Not up to Paix standards."

We lapse into silence and walk the periphery. I do not Feel anything, so I am unprepared when I stumble and fall to my knees.

"Lisle!" Sarta exclaims.

"I am unharmed," I say quickly and stand up. I rub my right knee. "I have stumbled over . . ."

I notice the shoe, then the leg. The shoe is Paix.

"Sarta," I whisper, then crouch beside the body.

It is a male Paix of higher spance, and his mouth is slack. One hand covers his eyes, and the other one still clutches the branch of a bush. "Has he fallen?"

Sarta shakes her head. "From where?" Sarta puts her hand over the Paix male's nose. "He is not Dead. His breath moves across my fingers."

"Surely, he cannot be asleep on the wet Earth by choice. Where is his companion? The Paix generally do not travel in Solitary."

Sarta walks in widening circles. "I do not see another."

I lean over the Paix male and open my mind. I Feel no weight, no connection. "He is not connected."

"What Aura is he?" Sarta asks and returns to the body.

I look at the male's shoes. "Yellow."

"How can he not be connected? The Paix only disconnect when they Cease. It is painful for them. Being Singular is like . . ."

I finish Sarta's sentence, "Finding you are the only one left in the Koja."

Rest.

My mind rings with chaotic noise. It is deafening. "They have found me," I scream and clasp my hands to my ears. I fall heavily to the ground. The Paix male rises and begins walking backward into the trees. I reach a hand toward him, and Sarta grabs his shoulder, but he shakes her off and continues lurching into the forest.

Disconnect. Depart. Lisle. Subject.

I press my hands tightly over my ears but cannot shut off the chaotic noise ripping through my mind.

Lisle. Lisle. Depart.

I do not understand.

"Stop!"

Depart. Disconnect. No.

I struggle to close the edges of my consciousness around myself, but the threads of Drifting are wrapped around me tightly. I scream so loudly that the threads finally snap when I Feel physical pain. I Drift back into my own mind, my own body.

"Lisle," Jaigon says and skids to a stop in front of me. He drops to his knees. Chur is directly behind him. He has the Lexicon out, Recording.

Sarta alternates between humming and babbling about the Paix male. Mon and Hasta arrive. Jaigon waves them away. "Go, search." He puts one hand over my mouth and the other behind my head. "You must stop screaming."

Shocked, I close my mouth. A bitter taste fills it. I had not realized I was still screaming. When I look at Jaigon, I see concern in his eyes.

Chur leans over me with the Lexicon. "Describe the scene."

I shake my head no.

Jaigon whispers to me. "Can you control your voice?"

I nod yes.

Jaigon removes his hand from my mouth. "Did the male harm you?"

"No."

"Did the Paix infiltrate your mind? Initiate connection?"

"Yes. The noise was . . . more than horrific. It was chaos."

Rastin's face looms above me. "The Indentured are all deactivated. One touched me. I believe he hugged me. It was awkward. What has passed here?"

"A Paix male, Yellow, was found by Sarta and Lisle. Apparently, he was disconnected. Then he reconnected, and Lisle witnessed it from the Paix viewpoint."

Sarta puts her hand on my forehead. "Did they hear you, Lisle?"

The only reason why the strings snapped was my scream. Pain separated me. "Yes. No. I do not know."

Jaigon is very still. "Sarta, go ask the group to return to the clearing."

Sarta rises and walks away from us. Jaigon strokes my hair. "Stay with me. How can they hear you on the periphery?"

"I was watching but could hear. The Paix was in me. They heard my pain. I was screaming. My throat closed off, then they let go of me."

Rastin nods. "It does make sense. You were acting as a Singular in that moment. As I was deactivating the Indentured, I realized how the disfunction of one can affect the disfunction of them all. The Paix has connected us all to the Ortus. We will all fail together."

Mon skids to a stop in front of us. She makes eye contact with me.

"I am functioning," I say.

Jaigon talks over me. "Do not underestimate yourself. Or the Auraless."

"I do not," Rastin says. "But the construction of the Yuan is beyond our mechanical capabilities. I can learn, but not that quickly."

"You make it sound like we are parasites," Mon says. "Your voice was a roar, Lilse."

"My mind was filled with noise. I wish it had been your music."

Jaigon walks in a circle, then stops. "The Paix entered your mind when you were sucked in by accident as the Paix male reconnected. You did not initiate the connection?"

"I did not," I respond. "And it was not connection. I was suddenly engulfed, and then I had to get out." I replay the experience in my head. I remember my mental cry for the voices to stop, then . . .

No.

I swallow. "They heard me. I am sure now."

Chur leans into my space. "They heard you. Please repeat for the Record."

"Yes."

Rastin shuffles his feet. "That is a first."

Jaigon paces, then stops short in front of us. "We continue on."

"Agreed," I say. "I wish to leave this place."

I take a direct route across the field to the Go-Go. I look at the Indentured as I walk by them. Many stand in groups, others alone. They are still and at peace, and I Feel a sense of collective rightness. When I reach the Go-Go, I climb in. The rest of the group follows me, and we take our places in silence.

"Our direction is across the clearing," Rastin says. "It is several kilometers before the first Tether, but I am sure it lies within that trajectory."

The Go-Go lifts and hovers across the field. I Feel regret. I am not sure what I have left in the clearing, but I know that something of me remains there.

CHAPTER 10

No contact was maintained with the Leadership, and the Indigo Children struggled to create a new society. Although the lower cliffs were defensible, food and shelter were scarce. Many died of hunger and exposure to the elements. The Indentured, the original high cliff dwellers who did not flee to the Tunnels, took many of the Indigo Children into their homes. They traded goods for services and co-habitated peacefully. Then the Golden Children were born, and with them, an even greater understanding of the Earth and how to utilize its bounty. They explored terra farming and technological innovations via their stronger collective consciousness.

—HISTORIES OF PAIX, INDIGO 4.1

W E REACH THE EDGE OF THE fine, gold sand that flanks Paix. The Helio has risen, but the light is hazy. Mist shrouds the short trees and rain sputters off and on. I have never seen the Earth so uncontrolled. "It is beautiful in this way. Free."

"It is disorganized," Rastin comments. "Not good for habitation."

I sigh. "But beautiful."

Sarta makes a derisive, clicking noise. I look at her in surprise. Her emotions are vague, indistinct. "What is wrong?"

"We must break the fast."

Jaigon changes the visual input setting on the console to a wider view. "We will. The First Tether."

I see the beginnings of the Paix buildings. They are square with the color of their residents' Aura displayed prominently on tall, sliding doors. The homes are connected via walkways over water and stone. Each one connects to the next in concentric rings, and there is a central . . .

Sarta makes a choking noise and turns away from the view screen.

I gasp. Some of the buildings are collapsed inward, as if a giant Being had stepped through their roofs. Doors are stripped of their color. Several walkways are piled on top of each other. "What has . . ."

Sarta places her hand over my mouth. She gestures to the sky through the view screen, and I see a cylindrical tube moving toward the Go-Go. It is shiny and turns counter-clockwise.

Jaigon leans over and pats the control panel. Rastin relinquishes his seat. Sarta takes it.

The cylindrical tube must be a Listener, though I have only seen them in historical documents stored in the Lexicon. They were presumed extinct machines.

Sarta says, "Now," and taps a sequence of images into the Go-Go. A burst of energy kicks the Go-Go back. A flash of light streaks in front of us. The cylindrical tube collides with it and disintegrates.

Jaigon puts his hand on Sarta's shoulder. "Nice work."

Chur Records. Hasta and Rastin stare at Sarta. Mon swings in from the back flip. "That was quite a ride. Good thing I am hooked in. What happened?"

"There could be more," Sarta says at the same time.

Jaigon taps Sarta's shoulder. She moves. "Park the Go-Go, Rastin."

Rastin returns to his seat and follows the command. His body language is stiff and uncomfortable.

"What was that?" Mon asks again.

"A Listener," I respond. "Sarta destroyed it somehow."

"Someone could have warned me," Mon says and looks at Hasta.

Hasta shrugs his shoulders.

Rastin turns around in the seat. "The Go-Go is parked. Explanation, please."

Jaigon and Sarta exchange glances. Jaigon answers. "Subject 32 was engaging in Gathering. There was discordance in the Paix's Lexicon about two months ago, and she brought it to my attention."

Mon whistles. "Els was Gathering? Like in the Fusion Wars? Spying?"

"Yes. The Lexicon was her specialty, and she came to me when she accidentally discovered Paix diagrams of Listeners embedded in the Lexicon over a month ago. It was perplexing, so I advised her to keep a careful watch. Gathering is the best description."

I shake my head. "No. They must have been Ancient diagrams."

"I saw the diagram myself. The technology and function is similar, but the materials are new. It is unclear if it was the Paix or the Ortus alone creating it via the Indentured."

"The Ortus does not act alone," Rastin says. "It is programmed to act for all."

"Not in this case," Jaigon continues. "Or, at least that is not what Subject 32 determined."

Rastin stands up. "I would like to see this diagram."

"Not accessible without the Paix Lexicons," Jaigon says. "But it was convincing. It is why I authorized the Gathering."

"You did not seek the counsel for this decision?" Mon asks.

"I did not" Jaigon replies. "I discussed it with Sarta. We decided the best course of action was to Gather and wait."

I sink back against the wall of the Go-Go. Nothing I know is real, and everything I Feel is false. "So, Listeners have been constructed for our specific elimination."

"No," Jaigon says. "There is no weaponry aboard these Listeners. They are for Listening. To us."

"We are the only speakers," Rastin concludes. "It would have been helpful to know you attached an energy supply beneath us. It is unsophisticated and quite dangerous."

"The risk had to be taken," Sarta interjects.

Rastin turns back to the view screen. "It could have blown the Go-Go up along with the Listener."

Mon pulls her flute from her bag and looks at it. Her fingers move over the holes. "The Ortus listens to us."

"And the Paix perish." Rastin changes the view screen to a close-up of the Paix housing. "This is purposeful destruction."

Jaigon steps away from the console. "We break the fast, then continue. Rastin, you will report on the damage after nourishment."

No one argues. Mon replaces her flute and digs in her pack for the small packet that contains our nutritional allotment. Mon unwraps hers and takes a bite. I watch her chew. She opens her mouth and makes a face. "Hey! You have to nourish. Get out your allotment."

I nod and pretend like I am fiddling around in my pack. I am in a daze. My mind is still wrapping around Jaigon's information. The Ortus is listening to us.

Disconnect. Leave. Depart.

I put my hand to my head and try to ignore the voice.

Disconnect. Leave. Depart.

"Are you the Ortus? Stop, stop!"

"Nourish," Mon says and taps my arm.

Mon is calm and beautiful. Her hair falls around her face like a dark waterfall, and she is smiling at me. It calms me to look at her. I return her smile. I pull out my nutritional allotment and peel off the colorless outer wrapper. It crinkles in my hand. I force myself to nourish. Each bite is tasteless, and I swallow slowly.

We complete our nourishment, and Rastin stands. He brushes the front of his shirt with his fingers and looks at the group.

"Report," Jaigon says.

"The homes have collapsed inwardly. The supporting infrastructure is non-functioning, so what is built around and over it will continue to crumble. It is a complete system breakdown from the inside out."

System Failure.

"Why? How? Who are you?"

"What a disaster," Hasta says. "The Ortus controls the temperature, the lighting, the stability of the Earth via the Yuan, and without regulation . . ."

Rastin completes Hasta's thought. "It all falls inward. It also explains the Koja's malfunction. The Ortus is in control."

Hasta snaps his fingers. "Collective planning. Not a good choice. No back up system."

"Then we correct the problem," Jaigon says. "We are the back up system. We split into specialties and search the first Tether for answers."

Rastin opens the portal, and Jaigon signals for us to leave the Go-Go. I am the last to leave the craft and close the door carefully behind me.

"You are to stay with me," Jaigon says. "I need you to open and Drift and detail anything that you Feel from the periphery. Specifically, the Ortus."

"I will."

We move away from the Go-Go in silence. The rain has stopped, and though the temperature is below average, it is no longer cold. I Drift but do not Feel a pressing weight. There is calmness around me, and the colors are crisp.

Jaigon is waiting for my report, so I say, "I Feel nothing. There is a harmonious presence around us."

"Let me know when that changes, even if it becomes more harmonious. I need to be aware of any change at all."

The others in our group separate, and I lose track of Hasta,

Sarta, and Chur. Mon and Rastin reach the first ruined home. Rastin crouches beside it and touches the frame of the building. Mon disappears around the side, but I hear her flute.

Jaigon and I continue to the next home in the Tether. Both doors are bright Orange. I wonder if the home belongs to Jooroo's family. I hope that it does not, as it is empty. Three other homes are built in this complex, and they are empty as well.

When we walk around to the central space between the four homes, two voices creep into my mind.

What is this? What are you? Where am I?

Disconnect. Depart.

Do not leave me. Where am I? Who am I? I am afraid.

Disconnect. Depart.

The voices are clear, distinctly separate entities. The second is not of the Paix. I stop walking. "The Singular connects to me. I have heard the voice a few times. And another voice, a stronger one."

I hear myself say the Words, then feel severe pain in my chest. I am no longer floating but pinned down. I shut my mind completely, and the pain recedes. It would be easy to stay in this strange mental space where nothing is—no Auraless, no Paix.

"Lisle," Jaigon says.

I do not know how many times Jaigon says my name. It brings me back from the edge of nothingness, and I finally answer. "Yes."

"What is a Singular?"

"One mind. Alone."

Jaigon continues to ask me questions, but I do not listen. Instead, I walk to the middle of the open space shared by the four houses and sit down. I Feel the presence of the Singular just outside of my reach, almost like a shadow.

I look around the space at the doors, and I do not Feel the Paix. Just the other voice. "The Singular is following us. The other voice is the Ortus. I am sure of it. There is one other voice, from my dream. It does not connect through me as often."

Jaigon sits in front of me. He touches my chin. I lean into his hand. "Explain this to me."

"There is a Singular that can enter my mind, and that of the Ortus, I think. It is now following us, or me, to be precise. The Ortus will not accept it."

"So, there are . . . two voices?" Jaigon asks.

"Yes, plus the third one. They are distinct. The Paix does not understand the Singular voice. The Ortus will not. My Father's voice is the third voice. Except it is not my Father's voice alone, but millions of voices."

"The Paix do not have voices."

"I know. But it is not exactly speech. It is in here," I tap my mind. "Thoughts made of Words."

"Many have evacuated," Hasta interrupts from behind me. I swivel to look at him.

"The rest?" Jaigon asks.

"Some did not heed the call. It is strange. It is like they just stopped in the middle of their daily routines. No signs of struggle. Most look like they are sleeping. Some have torn themselves apart and are no longer functioning."

"Leave them," Jaigon says quietly. Hasta walks away. Jaigon returns his gaze to me. "Is this Singular . . ."

"Malevolent?" I supply. "No and yes. It is Unsure. Volatile. The Ortus cannot control it. It connects, disconnects randomly. That is why it is rejected."

"Can you open to it again? Where does it come from? Is it another intelligence?"

"I wish I knew these answers. It will call to me again, and I will figure it out. It recognizes me and trusts me. I know that sounds crazy."

"It does not. It recognizes the sound of your mind, like I do your voice. You have a frequency."

"Yes. Exactly. And it knows that I am open. I do not hurt it."

The ground begins to shake. The water in the pool near us spills out onto the ground violently. Jaigon grabs my left arm right above the elbow. "Run!"

My feet move in rhythm with Jaigon's, but I struggle to keep up. The ground is snaking around us, and large fissures form in places. Water seeps up in the cracks. Trees disappear into the Earth as if grass and stone had become teeth and jaws.

I see a flash of light directly ahead of us. The Go-Go skims the surface of the trembling Earth. I trip and scrape the ground with my arm. Jaigon lifts me up. The ground falls away in front of us and Jaigon jumps over it, half carrying me. The Go-Go is sweeping towards us.

"Mon!" I cry and reach my arm back toward the first Tether, but Jaigon does not allow me to stop running. We reach the Go-Go. Jaigon lifts me through the portal. "Climb in."

"Mon!"

"Keep her in the Go-Go," Jaigon yells. Rastin pulls the front half of my body through the portal and forces me into the back of the Go-Go. He sits in the pilot seat. "Stay still so I can find her. Attempting escape will only hinder my search."

I look at my hands. My left hand is covered in dirt. The contrast between my hand and the clean whiteness of the Go-Go is stark. I look through the nearest wall. The world is in motion, trying to shake us off it. Everything is falling. I am Drifting.

Disconnect. Leave. Depart.

Is this the light?

"Come help me," Rastin says. His voice is panicked, and it brings me out of a fitful Drifting. "The ground is falling away too quickly for me to scan everywhere. I need your help now to find Mon and the others."

I scramble to stand behind Rastin's pilot chair. I scan the ground in the left corner of the view screen. Movement catches my eye. "There!"

"Hold on," Rastin says. He turns the Go-Go 180 degrees, then speeds toward the twelfth building of the Tether. Chur is standing in the middle of the clearing Recording, and Rastin hovers above him.

I force the portal open manually. "Come on!"

Chur drops the Recorder, and it rolls several feet away. He bends to retrieve it and falls to his knees. "Leave it!"

Chur does not listen, but he does hurry. He crawls to the Recorder, grabs it, and rolls to a crouch. He springs over a widening crack in the earth, lands on his feet, and grabs my right hand. I grasp a wall hand hold with my left hand and haul Chur in as far as I can. He is sweating, and there is fear in his eyes. "The underground structures are collapsing. There is water everywhere. Metal building pieces are flying around like giant, sharp leaves. I have it all Recorded."

I do not care about any of this. "Where is Mon?"

Chur drags himself the rest of the way in the Go-Go and blinks. "Oh. Mon is in the next Tether. Roof. I heard the flute before the eruptions."

Rastin starts flying even though the portal is open and creates drag. I manually hook the shoe holds around my ankle. I hook them around Chur's as well. I am ready when Rastin shouts, "Grab Mon's hands. Assist her, Chur."

I crawl and put my head and hands out the portal. Everything is upside down. The air is full of debris, but I focus on Mon. She is standing on the remains of a rooftop. Half of it is gone, and a river of swirling water engulfs most of the house. The doors to the home are open but still intact. The Yellow on them is peeling off in odd, striped patterns.

"Mon," I scream and reach for her hand. She grabs my right hand, and I secure the back of her pack with my left hand. The Go-Go lifts. A flat piece of metal hits the side of the Go-Go. It sounds like a deep gong. The Go-Go shakes, but continues rising. Chur wraps his arms around my torso and pulls.

"Put your foot on the landing gear," I say to Mon. "Climb over my back."

"Hurry," Rastin says. "I see Jaigon and Hasta."

Mon climbs over me, and I hear her feet hit the floor of the Go-Go with a heavy thud. Three seconds later, I see Hasta and

Jaigon waiting on a slim piece of land between two fissures. Hasta is bent over and holding his arm. Jaigon motions for Rastin to put down.

"I cannot," Rastin says. "Tell him, Lisle."

"He cannot put down!" I scream. Rastin levels the Go-Go over them, and I reach for Hasta. His eyes are wide and pain-filled. The world rumbles around me. It sounds as if every building is breaking apart. "Lift him to me."

Jaigon lifts Hasta, and I put my arms beneath his armpits and lock my hands. Hasta moans. "Chur, pull!"

Chur grabs my waist and pulls us back. Mon reaches over my body and drags Hasta in.

Hasta screams and flails. There is a gash on his head, and by the angle of his arm, I know that it is broken. I search for Jaigon's hands.

"Jaigon," I cry, as the Earth beneath him gives way. Jaigon grabs the landing gear of the Go-Go, and I inch forward so he can grab my left shoulder and arm. The shoe hold strap breaks, and I slide out of the portal.

Mon and Chur catch my legs inside the Go-Go, but for a moment, I am between in and out, and my only thought is how I wish to be in Jaigon's arms in the ocean again.

Disconnect. Leave. Depart.

"Help me."

Jaigon hoists himself over me and uses my body like a bridge. He is in the Go-Go before I can take another breath. My body is pulled into the Go-Go by someone, and I twist violently and sit on the Go-Go's floor. I hold my knees to me and try to remember what safety feels like. My hands tremble.

Jaigon is already standing next to Rastin. "Secure the portal, Mon. Get us out of here, Rastin."

"Sarta?" Rastin asks.

"She would not leave her parents. They were inanimate. We tried to pull her away, but the Earth gave way."

Mon latches the portal shut and sinks to her knees next to

Hasta. "We cannot just leave her."

"We depart. Hasta was struck by flying shrapnel because of her in the escape. She confessed to Els' murder."

What I have been Feeling in Sarta is guilt. I am shocked. "But why?"

"She would not tell me why."

Mon whimpers, and I hold more tightly to my knees.

"We speak her name no more," Jaigon continues. "No body, no Ritual. She killed her own."

I wince. "She loved her . . ."

"Enough," Jaigon says. "We continue. Rastin? Damage to the Go-Go?"

"Only cosmetic."

"Explanation of what we just witnessed?"

"I was right," Rastin comments in a hollow voice. "The Paix built over the plumbing and old subways of the Ancients. They are caving in without the Ortus to maintain the environmental controls. They will all be rubble soon."

"The end of us all," Chur says in a deep voice. "And I will be the one to Record it."

"Enough, Chur," Mon says. "Stop Recording."

"It is my duty."

"Jaigon?"

"We must keep a Record," Jaigon says. "But we must also remain calm. This is the first Tether. First, so hastily constructed. The other Tethers were not built in such a way. Perhaps it will not be so . . . devastated further in."

Mon leans over Hasta and puts her hand on his face. It is pale, and the gouge on the side of his head is deep and bleeding. She cradles his head in her lap. "None of that matters. I have no medical knowledge to assist Hasta."

"My arm is broken," Hasta whispers. "My ribs . . ."

Hasta's voice fails, and Jaigon crouches beside him. "Bind the arm to something flat and wash the head wound with disinfectant. Infection is the main concern. Bones heal. We continue to the Second Tether."

"Wash it with what?" Mon says pitifully. "There is no Replicator on the Go-Go."

Jaigon stands. "Lisle. Take Subject 1's water pack and give it to Mon. Assist her in the cleansing. Rastin, move the Go-Go to the second Tether."

"I do not know if the Go-Go will withstand the wind and make . . ." Rastin does not finish his sentence. Jaigon gives him a look that does not allow for argument.

Mon wipes Hasta's face with her shirt. The Go-Go lurches. Chur closes his eyes and straps both his feet in. I look through Sarta's pack. Her pack is empty except for her Lexicon and a spare shirt made of stiff, colorless fabric. I wonder if she knew that she was not returning to the Go-Go. I take the shirt out and close her pack. I dig in my pack and find my water.

The Go-Go is bouncing in air pockets, so I push myself across the Go-Go's floor to Mon and Hasta. "Use my ration of water. I never drink it all, anyway."

Mon takes it from me and uses a spare under covering from her pack to wipe off Hasta's forehead. I help her clean the gash on his forehead. "Tear his shirt on the side."

The material tears easily, and Mon feels around Hasta's chest and arm. Splotches of swelling and bruised flesh surround a bone protruding from his arm at a sickening angle.

I offer Mon Sarta's shirt. "Use this."

Mon tears a piece of cloth from Sarta's shirt to bind the wound. "The bone is definitely broken. He needs a proper binding. And he needs to be scanned by a Replicator to check for internal bleeding."

The Go-Go lurches violently, and though I do not scream, I want to. Our world is spinning out of control. "We have to bind the bone now."

"With what?"

Mon looks around the Go-Go's cabin. I look as well, but can think of nothing that could serve in this fashion.

"Use the back flip rail," Chur says. He is sweating. The Go-Go lurches again. He shuts his eyes and gags.

"Great idea." Mon disappears into the back flip. Jaigon kneels next to Hasta, whispers something, then pulls on Hasta's arm. Hasta gasps. I Feel pain radiating from him. It is so strong, my head begins to pound in response. After two more hard pulls, Jaigon completes the process. Hasta passes out.

Mon returns with the rail from the back flip. "It broke right off," Mon says triumphantly.

"I am not sure it is supposed to," Chur replies and grimaces as the Go-Go lurches to the side.

Mon hands the piece to Jaigon, and he slips it around the back of Hasta's shoulder and arm.

"He is not . . ."

"He has lost consciousness," Jaigon says. "Do not panic. I had to move the bone back into place, and it was . . ."

"Pain-filled," I say grimly and shiver.

"Give me a spare outer cover."

I pick up my pack and take out mine. It is black and sturdy. I hand it to Jaigon, and he rips it into four strips. He uses two strips to tie the rail to Hasta's arm. The other two, he uses to bind Hasta's arm across his chest so the shoulder is immobile.

"Provide comfort," Jaigon says and stands.

Mon looks scared. "Provide comfort," she repeats. I know it is a task that cannot be fulfilled properly. So does she.

Rastin stops the Go-Go and announces, "Second Tether."

We all peer out of the view screen. The Second Tether looks stable and unaffected. The doors on the individual homes are shut, and there are no damaged buildings. The colors are vibrant and the Earth calm. But there are no Paix outside.

"Continue to the Third Tether," Jaigon says. "These have been evacuated. Lisle?"

"Agreed. I Feel nothing. Continue to the Third Tether." After I say the Words, a sense of helplessness wraps me. I am floating in a field of stationary Indentured. They do not notice me. At the edge of the field, my parents are standing in the midst of other Paix. I raise my hand in greeting and run towards them, but my steps are slowed by questions from the Singular.

Who am I?

I stop, and all of the Paix's eyes close. "Who are you?" I ask.

Who are you? the voice echoes.

The voice is like water slipping through my fingers. "I am Lisle, Subject 46. Why are you hurting my people?"

My people? the voice echoes.

"They are my Parents," I cry desperately. "Why are you hurting them?"

Parents the voice says and pulls away. I reach for the voice. I am swimming in a pool of bodiless voices, and then a sense of serenity enfolds me.

The Ortus I hear, and then my Mother's eyes are in mine. Rest.

"Please," I cry. "I do not understand."

Lisle.

I hear my name clearly before my thoughts dissipate like tiny balloons into the floor of the Go-Go. I know what the Ortus wants. I survey the Go-Go with new eyes. Hasta is lying on the floor, and Rastin is desperately trying to steer the Go-Go. We are tilted, and smoke covers the view screen.

Mon grasps my arm. "You were glowing. It is not a suggestion. You were."

"I know," I say calmly. "Everything is fine now."

"She wakes," Jaigon says. "Hold the course."

"We must abandon ship. I cannot . . ." Rastin stops speaking.

The Go-Go rights itself, and the view screen clears.

Everyone stares at me.

For once, I know exactly what to say. "I understand the problem. There is a Singular, and an Ortus, and they are not compatible. The answers lie in the Ortus. We have to find a way to tap into its programming."

"Tap into it how?" Jaigon asks.

"It is a system failure. What would we do if that happened at the Koja?" I ask.

"We evacuated."

Jaigon is frustrated, I Feel it. "But if we did not evacuate, what then?"

"Re-engage the programs? Rastin?"

"A complete reset of the Ortus is not illogical," Rastin says. "If we can determine how to do that without Hasta."

I know this answer is right. "It is the only way."

Jaigon takes a deep breath. "Then we will go. Rastin, do you know the co-ordinates of the Ortus?"

"I know roughly where it is. We all do. But I do not know what the Ortus will be like. The entire building could be falling apart. For the programming to fail this much, the Ortus may already be in complete ruin, barely functioning, and we will be . . ."

"Going there," Chur interrupts. "I concur with Lisle. This is the only logical path left to us. We cannot just keep going from Tether to Tether. It serves no purpose."

"What are we to do about Hasta?" Mon asks and returns to his side.

"We will find a working Replicator near the Ortus," Jaigon responds.

"If there is one." Chur stops typing and looks at me. "Just to confirm. You Feel the Singular within your mind? Mixed with the Ortus?"

"I did. And my parents—the Paix. There are three voices. Three view points that do not mix exactly."

"Then you are a hybrid. A true hybrid. All can connect to you. I did not think I would see this day."

"None of us did," Mon says and strokes the side of Hasta's face.

"I am not a hybrid. I am just Lilse."

"But . . ."

Jaigon motions for Chur to be silent. He complies.

Hasta opens his eyes. "We will find you care," I say. I offer him water. "Drink."

Hasta refuses the water. Mon lets Hasta's head rest on her pack and moves beside me. "I am afraid."

The Go-Go changes direction. "Do not be. I feel a greater sense of stability the closer we get to the Ortus."

Mon puts her head on my shoulder. I hope that I am right.

CHAPTER 11

*After several hundred spances, terra farming was in place and flour-
ished. The Golden Children further developed 5D printing and the
Ortus, which was programmed to store all collective consciousness.
Replicators provided for their society's needs. The Indentured continued to provide services, but did not inter-marry with the Indigo
Children. Years of peace came, and the Indigo Children called the
new society Paix, or peace, from an Ancient language salvaged from
the Histories.*

—HISTORIES OF PAIX, INDIGO 4.2

P AIX LOOKS LIFELESS. THE colors are faded, as if the rain
has washed away their shine. I barely recognize the layouts
of the Tethers. The houses are jumbled pieces of other complexes
merged with existing structures.

We pass over another flooded Tether, and I try to analyze why
the water system has failed. "Rastin, is everything—mechanical
or not—reliant on Paix collective thought filtered through the
Ortus?"

"Everything runs through the Ortus."

"By design?"

"Yes. It is not ideal. Too much power in one place."

I consider Rastin's Words. "How could this have happened?"

"To a highly organized society, you mean?"

"Yes. It is like only eating one thing all the time. Why would any person want to do that?"

"We do that on specific days of the week. Each color has its fare."

"Yes, but we also have our gardens. We supplement the regular food supply."

Rastin squints. "Think of it this way. The Ortus combines the opinions of the Paix and determines one answer to a problem. For instance—how hot should the water be? If there is one Singularity that will not comply with an average degree answer, then the Ortus cannot quantify the answer and will reject all the answers until the Singularity is removed. There can be no round in a room constructed of squares."

I envision a room made entirely of right angles. It is not appealing. "So without complete accord, nothing is accomplished?"

"Depending on the programming of the Ortus. The water would run the gamut of temperatures given or not run at all. From what we have seen, I think it is the latter option."

Chur Records our conversation. "How are you going to tap into the Ortus without a working Paix Lexicon?"

"I am considering a plan," Rastin says. "I think Lisle should consider her plan as well."

"My plan?" I say in a faltering voice.

"Do you have any thoughts?"

I shake my head no. Jaigon holds his hand up suddenly in the Paix symbol for silence—a closed fist with his thumb sticking up between the third and fourth fingers. I straighten my shoulders and prepare for whatever will happen. Rastin stands swiftly, and Jaigon sits down in the pilot's seat.

I tense and wait for the flash of light. I hear my heart beating in my inner ear. After several long seconds, Jaigon stands and motions for Rastin to retake the controls.

"A Listener?" I ask.

"No," Jaigon says. "See for yourself."

I look out the view screen. A light orb is flashing to the left of the Go-Go. It is not connected to a roof, and its motions are erratic.

"How did it . . . oh." I realize that the entire Tether is without affixed light orbs. Most float in the air randomly. Many have fallen into the houses, and weak flashes occur every second. Normally, the light orbs mark Paix homes and reflect the occupants' Auras and status. They are even more beautiful now that they are floating. The entire Tether is blinking as if to beckon our Go-Go forward.

"An example of the continual degradation of Ortus-controlled structures," Rastin says and turns the Go-Go to avoid a light orb.

Something shakes the Go-Go, and I stumble and clutch the hand hold to my left. It is a jarring sensation. Rastin bends over the controls, and I right myself. "Secure your Beings. We are in a pocket of strong wind currents."

The Go-Go shudders. I cannot believe that wind this strong is possible even with the degradation of the Yuan. I wonder how the Ancients and Befores survived. The sky cracks open, and a vein that looks like running fire slices to the ground. A loud noise booms through the Go-Go, and I fall to my knees and cover my ears. The Go-Go is moved suddenly to the right, then levels out.

"Remarkable," Rastin says calmly. "The amount of power in that lightning could be a source of energy for us if the Yuan fails. The trick would be to harness it, obviously."

Torrential rain pelts the Go-Go. Colors fade into black, and a buzz grows in my mind. I do not want to die this way. "Land, Rastin," I choke out. "The Ortus is unstable—I Feel it."

"If I can just get some data on that lightning . . ."

Jaigon does not let Rastin finish his sentence. "Land the Go-Go. We will use the time to find a Replicator."

Chur's Lexicon makes a high chirping sound. He mutters to himself. "The information needs to be downloaded into a larger storage facility. I cannot access either the Auraless or Paix repositories. I can Record no more until I store what I have."

The Go-Go drops several feet, and I clutch my stomach. Chur looks crushed, and his face pales. I want to help him. "You can use my Paix Lexicon. It does not function, but there is adequate storage space. I do not save most of the data I show my parents."

"Why not?" Rastin asks curiously. "It is your own private Record."

I shrug my shoulders. "I consistently make new data. The old is already done. I am sure there is adequate space, Chur."

"Yes, thank you. We cannot lose any of this data. I will need to make the transfer. Can I have it now? I do not want to miss anything important."

I retrieve the Lexicon from my pack. I hand the only remaining link to my parents to Chur. He begins the process of syncing the devices.

I return my focus to the view screen. Nothing looks familiar. Rain pelts the Earth, and the colors on the houses in the Tether are not vibrant. Everything is a shade lighter than what I remember.

Where are you?

"Not now."

I am confused.

I rub my eyes and tune the voice out.

Jaigon's hand closes over mine. It is cool on my flesh and comforting. We do not speak Words, but I Feel that he will lead us until the very end. He will be with me until the very end. He lets go of my hand, but the unspoken promise lingers between us.

"We approach the Tether," Rastin says. "This is my Strand. There is a Replicator in the main meeting area. Mon and Lisle's Strand lies further to the South. I can land here."

Another crack of lightning streaks across the sky.

"Excellent," Jaigon responds. "I will ready the landing gear. Prepare to tie down."

I sit down by Mon. The floor of the Go-Go is smooth, and I run my hands across it. "Almost home. You care for him?"

Mon looks up at me. "You can Feel what I Feel."

"I can. But I am asking."

Mon brushes the hair away from Hasta's eyes. "I do. I did not realize it until now. I hope it is not too late."

I hug Mon and leave my arm around her shoulders. The Go-Go lurches. I take a deep breath. Paix looks as if it is made of stone. I see no color, smell no scent. The Go-Go slows down and begins to descend. We swing in the wind like a ball on a string.

"This spot looks promising," Rastin says. "Hold on."

"I have completed the download," Chur says and hands me my Lexicon. His hands are shaky. "Please make sure it is safely stored. Every Recording is precious."

I take the Lexicon from Chur and tie it carefully in my pack. I am not sure what safe is anymore. The floor of the Go-Go separates me from the Earth beneath. I see it as stable and steady, and yet it is being pushed around in this volatile space.

"This is as close as I can get," Rastin says.

Jaigon is ready with the landing gear. "No one comes out until I have surveyed. Chur, you are with me."

Jaigon and Chur jump out of the Go-Go's portal. I Feel Chur's relief. He is motion sick. Mon whispers to Hasta, and Rastin remains at the controls.

I close my eyes and imagine that I am with my parents in their home. Mon has come over for a visitation, and we chat as my parents watch us. After a while, Mother prepares our favorite Paix meal in the Replicator—potatoes and vegetables with Paix rainbow sauce—and we all sit down at the table.

Mon and I do not speak through the meal, but I can tell that Mother and Father are. Mother's face relaxes into a smile every so often, and Father raises his eyebrows. I sop up the sauce with the potatoes until my plate is clean. After the meal, Mon and I gather the plates and cutlery, wash all of them, then return them to the Replicator. They disappear particle by particle. Mother and Father retire to the living room and sit on their Rumination rugs. Mon and I sit near them and close our eyes.

Rastin's voice breaks through my thoughts. "Lisle, they need you."

I open my eyes, and Rastin is standing over me. The tips of his black scarf hang in front of my eyes. I think of Joo-roo and hope he has not traveled to the Far yet.

"Jaigon has motioned for you to join them."

Cold. Here. Where are you? Where am I?

"Lisle! Jaigon is waiting for you," Mon says and pulls on my shirt sleeve.

"I do not know where you are. What are you?"

"I was thinking about visiting my parents years ago," I say quickly. "With you, Mon. I am going now."

I jump through the portal. It is a six foot drop to the Earth. The wind whips my hair, and rain pools in my eyes. I shiver, but I feel alive. The Earth smells pungent. I find Jaigon and Chur and walk towards them.

Jaigon holds a light orb on the tip of his fingers. Chur leans over the Replicator in the center of the square, and I can tell that something is wrong. The Earth sinks beneath my feet, and mud splatters my pants.

Jaigon addresses me, "Do your parents have this kind of Replicator?"

The outer casing is different—rainbow colored instead of red—but the symbols on the pad that opens the docking area are the same—lines in various concentric patterns. "Yes, it has the same symbols. Mother and Father had this visual kind installed so that I could help with the meals during preparation and cleanup."

"We are in gold Tether, blue Strand, so it would make sense that they would use this kind of styling," Chur says. He shields his Recorder from the rain with his shirt. "It is their preference for visual stimulation."

"Can you input Hasta's condition?" Jaigon asks. "I want to test the scanner. It keeps resetting to play music when I try."

Rain squeezes through the driest part of my clothing. My skin is clammy, and my hair drips down the back of my shirt. I press the pattern for a glass of water into the Replicator. Music plays—the soft, ethereal kind that filters into my parents' house when they are sleeping. I input the pattern a second time. Music continues to play.

I do not try a third time because the sky rends itself open and rain pelts us. "It is not functioning. Can we find one in a home? I am more familiar with the smaller ones."

Jaigon raises his eyebrows. "Are you sure?"

I am not sure, but the heavy rain is untenable. I half run to the second house in the courtyard. "Blue door. Maybe more in tune with us." I move my hand across the sensor. Nothing happens. I lean against the door and slide it slowly to the side.

"Careful," Jaigon whispers and nudges me forward. "Let us be quick."

I step over the threshold and peer into the home. It is just like my parents' home, except all of the furniture is blue. A sofa and two chairs are in the center of a lowered living room area. Blue cloth covers the wall. Silver stars are woven into the material. The round bedroom doorway is directly to the left of the living area. The kitchen and Ablution area are on the right. The kitchen is bright white with blue fixtures.

It is cold in the home, but at least we are sheltered from the rain. I sweep my hand to the right, and the lights come on.

"That is a good sign," Chur says.

I move into the kitchen and investigate to the right of the preparation table. I sigh in relief. A Replicator. Every Paix home is constructed with a similar floor plan, and the Replicator is exactly where it is in my Mother and Father's home.

"Lisle!" Jaigon says in a loud voice.

I turn, but Chur is inexplicably right in front of me. He pushes me to the side. "I have to Record."

There is a compact figure leering at us. Jaigon and Chur block my view, but it is a Paix male. The Paix male seems lost and keeps lashing out blindly. Jaigon stops his punches easily and puts the Paix male's arm behind his back. The male crumples to the ground.

I protest. "This is his home. At least gesture an apology. We are intruding..."

Chur steps wildly in front of me and catches a Paix woman running towards me. She has a scissor for plant cutting in her right hand.

Chur holds her by the waist, but she waves the scissors dangerously. I grab her wrist and shake it. She does not let the scissors go. "Please, we mean you no harm," I say as calmly as possible. "You—the Paix—are not well."

The Paix female's mouth twists. Her eyes are wild and unfocused, and I do not see her color at first. I peer into her eyes and find the colored rim.

"Gold," I squeeze harder on her wrist. "You do not belong in this home." Her eyes widen in surprise and then change. Now they are rimmed with blue. Her hair is short and almost white, it is so fair. I step away from the female. "Her Aura is changing."

Her left foot connects with my shin, and I feel pain, but she drops the scissors to the ground. I reach down for them and pick them up. She grabs a handful of my hair and pulls, and I strike out hard with my right arm.

The woman stiffens, then slumps over onto Chur's shoulder. "You have hit her, and she is unconscious," Chur says in astonishment.

I look at the woman, then at my hand. Shame washes over me. I taste bile in the back of my throat. "I did not mean to. She had my hair in her fist, and I merely..."

"See to the Replicator," Jaigon says and takes the woman's body from Chur. "That is most important. Chur, help me secure them."

Struggle. System failure. Rest.

"Her Aura was changing. Her eyes were not colored, then they were gold, then blue. And I . . ."

"Later," Jaigon says forcefully. He and Chur work to tie the couple to the couch. "The Replicator—Hasta needs us."

I retrace my steps to the Replicator. The Replicator's docking platform is lit, so I know that it is functioning. I put my hands on the input pad and punch in the pattern for vegetables and potatoes with Paix rainbow sauce. I order four servings.

The Replicator buzzes acceptance. A blue plate appears with potatoes and vegetables on it. Cutlery is attached to the side of the dish. There is less sauce than usual, but it smells and looks normal. "It works," I say softly and remove the plate.

"What are you doing?" Jaigon asks.

I hand Jaigon the plate. "I inputted what I remember best and the quantity. Here is the second plate."

I hand the second plate to Jaigon. He places it on the glass table on top of a blue serving tray. "How many did you request? We do not have time to consume this."

"Four." I take the third plate from the Replicator and wait for the fourth. "It is what I always order with my parents. Four for when Mon eats with us—which is when I have to help the most."

"I will eat," Chur says and takes the third plate from me. He takes a bite and grimaces. "I have never liked rainbow sauce. Too bland."

Jaigon watches Chur eat. "If it will create foodstuffs, then it will scan without malfunction."

"That is why I inputted something I knew multiple times. To test it."

Chur finishes the plate. "Not bad, all in all. Thank you."

I take the empty plate from Chur and return it to the Replicator. "As soon as we reload the Replicator, then it will reset itself, and I know what to do to access the scanner. Father showed me the pattern in case I ever harmed myself."

Jaigon looks over my head at the Paix couple on the sofa. His face is soft and wistful. "Few of us have such close contact with our Paix family. This must be difficult for you. Stay—I will bring Hasta to you."

Jaigon leaves. Chur takes another plate of food and eats. Rainbow sauce dribbles down his chin. "It will save the food in our packs. Who knows how long we will be on rations after this."

I pass my hand over a shallow drawer near the Replicator, and it pops open. I select a napkin and hand it to Chur. The drawer shuts by itself as it normally does.

"Gratitude." Chur wipes his mouth. "You should eat."

"You are right." I take one of the plates from the table and push the food around with the attached fork. The drawer pops back open. I put the plate down and push the drawer shut. "I am just not hungry."

"Not hungry, or cannot eat?"

"Cannot eat. I still see the eyes of the Paix female looking at me with hatred."

"Your reflexes were impressive."

"I struck another Being. Is it Recorded?"

"It is." Chur unzips his jacket. "It is warm in here."

I do not ask Chur to delete the Recording, as I know that he will not. History is too important to him. I wish it were not. I scrape my food into one of the remaining full plates. Sauce drips down the side, and I wipe it up with Chur's napkin. I do not want to leave a mess. I wash the plate and return it to the Replicator. "I hope Jaigon hurries. So far, so good."

Chur sits on a chair facing the Paix couple. He takes his jacket off and lays it across his lap. "I realize now the importance of Hasta's research on personal communication devices. We need to be better connected. Like them."

Hasta has been working on a means of communicating verbally without Paix technology across long distances. The Ancients had a similar device. If it works, then it would revolutionize the Auraless's lives—and I would know why Jaigon is taking so long.

Chur takes off his shoes. He looks closely at the contained

Paix. "To speak or not to speak. We have no choice. But they do."

Chur's voice sounds odd. I Feel meanness with him, a general detachment that was not there before. There are droplets of sweat near his hairline. His eyes are half closed. His jacket falls from his lap onto the floor. The Paix color wheel covers the back of it.

He drums his fingers on his knees, then places the Lexicon on the table. "Perhaps this experience will change the Paix. Perhaps not. Are they even Beings? They have collectively more faces, feet, and fingers than I can count."

"They are Beings. They are our parents."

"Superfluous. How many?"

Chur bounces his knees up and down. I answer slowly. "I cannot fathom the answer, Chur."

Chur laughs. The pitch is high and grating. "Good thing I know the answer to my own question. There is a census done every year during the Junkanoo. There is an exact number of Paix on Record."

"I know of the festival," I say calmly. Chur's left foot taps the floor. Sweat runs across his forehead. "I have never studied the census. The Ortus . . ."

"The Ortus," Chur interrupts and laughs. "The Ortus knows all—even before it is counted."

Chur walks around the sofa table and stares into the face of the male Paix. "And yet, we do not. We could retrain their minds. Remind them of their ability to speak. Show them the errors of the collective. Become their teachers, their masters."

"You speak of subjugation." Chur's eyes are red and watering. They look almost translucent. "Are you well? Perhaps you should sit?"

Chur takes his shirt off and looks at the Lexicon resting on the table. "I have never felt better. Look around, Lisle! Everything of value is stored in here. But what is it worth?" Chur's hands tremble. "What is it worth, I ask you? Answer me."

"Chur, you are not . . ."

"Do not tell me what I am not! My whole Being, my whole

life, they have told me what I am."

I back away. "You are Chur. Our brother."

"No, no, no," Chur says and laughs. Mucus hangs from his nostrils, and white spittle flies when he speaks. "You are one of them. I know it. I have seen your Aura. This whole exercise . . . it is for you. A test!"

I can back up no further—the preparation table is behind me. I pick up the Paix female's scissors from the counter. "I do not know of what you speak."

Chur unfastens the hooks on his pants. They fall, and he steps out of them. "Of course, you do. You know their plans. You are part of their plans. You must be."

Sweat rolls down Chur's body, and I look from his bare chest to his face. His under garments cling to his body. "I know only what you know of their plans. We journey together to find the source of the problem."

"No, no, no!" Chur screams. The scream ends in a fit of choking laughter. He picks up the Lexicon and walks to stand in front of me.

"Lisle," Chur says. His voice is full of hatred. "Subject . . . whatever your subject number is."

"46." I Feel Chur's emotions turn to rage.

"Yes," Chur says and waves the Lexicon in front of my face wildly. "Subject 46. This is the end of our existence. All Recorded on this device. Left here while I become . . . become . . ."

I Feel threatened and take action. I throw my body against Chur. He stumbles, and I take the Lexicon from him and run past him toward the door. I push hard, but it does not open. Chur's breath is on my neck, and his arm catches me underneath the chin.

"I will have you, Subject 46."

"No," I scream and stab at his arm with the scissors. He cries out in pain, and I lunge against the door again.

"Open!" I scream and pound on the door. It does not open. Chur grabs my waist and forces my chin up.

"You will pay for their misdeeds," Chur screams. "Not me. Not us."

"OPEN!"

I scream, but no Words come from my mouth. They come from my mind.

The door opens, and I fall through it. Chur falls with me. I stab him again with the scissors. They lodge in his flesh, so I let them go.

Chur grunts, and I twist away from him. I hold the Lexicon in my left hand and take the brunt of the fall with my right shoulder and side. I roll and maneuver myself back into the Paix home. The door shuts behind me.

I slump against the door cradling the Lexicon. My right hand is covered in blood. I look in horror at the Paix female, but her eyes remain lifeless, immobile. A shrill, ringing sound is painfully loud in my head.

Depart. Disconnect.

Chur bangs on the door. "You will destroy us. You deceiver. We will never be . . ."

Where am I? I feel . . .

Disconnect.

System failure.

I wipe the blood off on my pants and brace myself against the door.

"Help me."

A switch flips in my mind, and my head clears instantly. The home smells like potatoes and vegetables. Chur's blood is smeared across the Lexicon's screen, and I look at it as if I have never seen it before.

The female Paix stirs. Her eyes are every color of the rainbow. They dart from side to side, and she moans. I Feel sorry for her. "Rest. You want to rest."

Her eyes clear for a moment, and they are yellow. I reach my hand out to her, but she snarls. I am sad. "You know what is to come."

I hear a loud thud against the door, then silence. Sweat trickles down the inside of my arms, and I begin to shake. I press my face against the door.

"Lisle, open the door."

I know that it is Jaigon's voice. I feel his presence. "Chur has lost his sanity."

"Chur is disabled," Jaigon replies. There are several scratching sounds at the door, and then silence. "He will not hurt you now."

"Is he dead?" I curl my hand around the Lexicon. I make sure that I have a good grip on it. Chur would have wanted me to save it.

"Yes," Jaigon says. I can barely make out his words through the door. "I think that he has been poisoned. Did you poison him?"

I stand up and put the Lexicon in my pocket. It is too big and falls out. I pick it up and stuff it in my waistband. "I did not. I inputed the exact pattern into the Replicator . . ."

"Did you eat any of the replicated food?" Jaigon asks. "Open the door."

"Open."

The door opens. Jaigon rushes through it. I back away instinctively. There are scratch marks on his neck. "Are you all right?"

"Yes. The food is poisoned, Jaigon. We cannot use the Replicator to heal Hasta."

Jaigon surveys the room. His gaze settles on the sofa. "Are the Paix couple harmed?"

I shake my head no.

Depart. Leave. Disconnect.

A deep grumble comes from beneath us. Jaigon grabs my hand, and we run through the door as it closes. I trip over Chur's body. Blood pools from his mouth. We run off the porch, through the courtyard, and into the clearing beyond the Strand. Mon waves frantically at us from the Go-Go's portal.

"Too late," I whisper, but keep running towards the Go-Go because I know that I cannot stop running. I feel the weight of a thousand minds behind me, pushing me, fueling me to continue. They wish to rest.

Jaigon reaches the Go-Go and turns to me. His body language changes. I already know what he sees behind me. My legs pump into the ground. Sweat pools around my lower back. Jaigon climbs into the Go-Go, and it lifts.

There is no time for me.

"I will just keep running." I say to myself and look beyond the hovering Go-Go. In my heart, I know the Ortus will not let me go. It will use me. I connected this time—the door had opened to my mental command. I am Paix, if only briefly. I should Feel joy, but I Feel nothing.

The Go-Go stutters in the air, and I run past it. Jaigon calls my name. His hand is outstretched for me. He waits for me, but I know that the minds are behind me, and they have been directed to want me, not the others.

The Ortus wants me, and the Paix must obey.

Rest.

I have to keep running. I do not understand all the pieces yet, and the Ortus would overwhelm me, program me. The Auraless would suffer, the Paix, the Singularity.

The edge of the cliff rises, gold and red like blood mixed with the Helio. I do not slow down as I run off the edge of the cliff into the embrace of the air.

I am airborne. I see the ocean again and the edge of the known Earth. The Yuan rises like a thin, crescent bubble before me. I close my eyes and think of my Father, my Mother, Mon . . . Jaigon . . .

"I am Auraless!"

CHAPTER 12

The Ortus, which every Lexicon is connected to, holds all the knowledge the Paix carried from the cities to the tunnels. It also holds all current knowledge and thoughts of deceased and living Paix. The Paix continues to add to its knowledge daily.

—HISTORIES OF PAIX, INDIGO 4.4

T HE AIR TASTES SWEET IN my mouth, and I gulp its richness down. "Life," I whisper and throw my arms out wide as if to hold it all to me for the split second I am suspended in the air before I fall. It was worth living—without an Aura.

Something hard wraps around my waist, and my descent is stopped short. Steel wire bites into the flesh of my rib cage, pressing the breath from me. I gasp. My arms flail in front of me. I spin like a spider on the end of a string.

The Go-Go hovers above me. The gears of the towing apparatus strain to pull me in. Below me, bodies fall down the cliff soundlessly.

"Stop! Stop!" I scream. The Paix do not listen and continue to run off the cliff. The steel wire cuts harshly into my skin. "Stop!

You will not rest!" I yell until I have no more breath to yell with.

"STOP," I scream mentally, but with no effect.

"Lisle. Give me your hand."

I twist. The steel wire slices my flesh. I am slipping through its noose, and it would be so easy to fall with the Paix.

"Give me your hands," Jaigon shouts. I look up. Jaigon's eyes are beautiful, and I see myself reflected in them, a fragile body on a quivering string. "Do not leave me. Not now, Lisle. Please."

I reach to him with my left hand, and he grabs it. He hauls me in and lifts me into the bottom of the Go-Go. Jaigon wraps his hands around my shoulders and waist. He disconnects the steel wire. My body is between his legs like a child. His lips press mine. I do not flinch away. They are hard against my mouth, groping. His clothes feel rough, and I stroke his shoulders with my hands. Jaigon's fingers move against my neck, then trail down my body.

Jaigon moves his lips from mine and looks into my eyes. "Enough."

I nod my head yes. "Enough."

Mon kneels beside us. Mon unbuttons my shirt and looks at my flesh. She touches where it is cut underneath the armpits. "What were you thinking?"

Jaigon lets me go. He is sweating. "Have you lost your sanity? You ran off the edge of a cliff. I watched you run off the edge of a cliff."

"We all did," Mon says. She closes my shirt and presses her hand to my face.

"Yes, I did. I was drawing them away from the Go-Go so you could escape. I do not know what the Ortus wants and did not want to jeopardize our mission. But you caught me."

"If this Go-Go was not a work Go-Go, then it would not have had a cargo arm for boulder and tree removal, and we would not have," Jaigon says roughly.

"But it did."

"Rastin had this plan, and that is why he lifted up before you could board. Did you know that?"

"No."

Jaigon turns from me. I Feel his terror and am sorry that I have caused him to Feel this way.

"You were like a silver streak," Mon says.

I remember what I have learned. "Yes. I was in the collective. The Ortus is in control, not the Paix."

"You were in the collective," Mon repeats. "And you have returned."

"Yes."

The Go-Go jerks to the right. Jaigon drops to his knees and whispers, "It is of no matter. We will see this through. Together."

"I chose you. Over them."

Jaigon's eyes change, and I almost see color in them. "I know you did. I hope you always do. Bring us to the Ortus, Rastin."

"It is time to realize it. To be myself."

I say the Words clearly in my mind. I hope the Ortus, the Paix, the Singular—I hope everyone hears me. They have to hear me.

Mon grasps my hand. "Here . . . until the end. The very, very end."

"I know. Hasta?"

"He still has a fever. I am so grateful we had not moved him yet. Jaigon thought something was off."

"It was. I am sorry it did not work."

"I know," Mon replies and chews her lip. "I do not know what else to do. I did not realize how much I . . ."

Mon breaks off her words, and I stroke her hair. I have a quick vision of her and me playing in the forest near the Koja when we were younger helds. She has flowers in her hair, and she is laughing.

Mon is speaking to me, but I do not hear her. Colors stream from her lips and bend around her. A bubble forms around her, and it is iridescent and beautiful.

Disconnect. Depart. Leave.

"No."

"Lisle? What is happening to you?"

I look at Mon tenderly. I take the Lexicon from my waistband. It is intact. "Nothing. Chur's work is saved. Our story is saved. Mon, you Record now."

"But Hasta . . ."

"Watching Hasta get weaker will not aid in his recovery," Jaigon says. "Record."

Mon takes the Lexicon. "Is it just like our personal ones?"

"Yes." I consider Mon. She is not the same when she is in motion. She has color—sometimes red, sometimes blue. It is like seeing through a prism. "Hold still. I can almost see . . ."

"Color?" Rastin asks. He maneuvers the Go-Go around a jutting promontory. At our rate of speed, it is impressive that he does not hit the nearest rock formation as he swings dangerously around it. "An Aura?"

"Yes. And no."

Mon's eyes are wide. "What kind of Aura?"

"Not an Aura. You have color. Like color energy is wrapped around you and can only be seen when it is moved. How did you know, Rastin?"

"You have touched the collective mind," Rastin says. "It is like a circuit. Open, shut. Once used, the circuit remembers the pathway. On both sides. I did not realize it was motion dependent. It may not be for true Paix."

"But for me . . ."

"That is how you see it."

The explanation seems reasonable, and yet, I am not content. "So, I sort of see as they see? Forever?"

"I am not sure. It is just a theory."

"But you look the same."

"Do I?" Rastin asks. "Look again."

I look at him more closely, and something clicks in my perception. I see right through him instead of around him.

"Oh." Rastin truly is colorless. He is completely without color. I look back at Mon. She shimmers with a golden hue, but her body is colorless. Color moves around her, in her, through her.

I do not look at Jaigon for fear of what I may see if I really look.

"I do not," Rastin says. "I figured as much. Are we monochromatic?"

Jaigon sucks in his breath, but I still do not look at him. "No, not monochromatic. Mon is colorless, but with a golden shimmer. As she moves, her energy takes on different hues. You are colorless, Rastin. No shimmer."

"I see," Rastin says, then chuckles.

"What do I look like?" Jaigon asks. He puts his hand under my chin and pulls upward. "Your eyes are so light now. Tell me what I look like."

I look at Jaigon. There is an energy, a deep, burgundy color shimmering within him that is unlike Mon's or Rastin's. It moves inwardly as his emotions change. "Energy."

"The Paix sees me as energetic. That is comforting."

"No. You have color, an energy, but it is not a shimmer. It is inside you."

"What does . . ."

"Does not matter," Rastin interrupts. "We can sort this out later. I am having trouble navigating in this weather, so for now, let us stick to solving this mystery. Seeing this way is the key to the Ortus."

"How?" I ask.

"The Ortus is programmed to see in color."

"But the Ortus does not see. It is a machine," Mon says.

Rastin rights the Go-Go. "It recognizes how those of the Paix see and think. The recognition is based on how you see yourself. Look at your hands, Lilse. What do you see?"

I put my hands in front of my eyes, and I really look at them. They are my hands, but different. They glow silver.

"Oh," I say and take a deep breath. "Oh my."

"I thought so. The Ortus will allow you to connect. I hope."

"But my eyes have not changed completely."

"Irrelevant. The Aura may be abnormal, but it is still there. Think of it as a half Aura."

I study my hands again. They look like I have dipped them in silver light. I have always wanted an Aura, worked for an Aura, and now that I have one—a half, strange one though it may be—I do not want it.

I voice my Feelings aloud. "I do not want this."

Rastin changes the Go-Go's view screen magnification. The Paix is wide and large. "It is what you are."

"I am Auraless."

Jaigon puts his hand on my shoulder. "Not anymore. But perhaps we are not either. You see us in color, and that may be what we truly are. Now you see it."

Mon agrees. "We are family, however we see. But why would the Ortus accept her, half Aura or not? She is not Paix."

"She is alike enough. Every machine wants to continue its programmed operations. Think of the Indentured. The Ortus is no exception."

"So, it has been aiding our plight," I say. "Helping with the Go-Go, allowing me to Drift in and out. Connecting to me. Keeping parts of the Paix functioning in hopes that we will reach it and fix the Singularity."

"Yes," Rastin says. "It needs you. What is this?"

We all look through the view screen. Flocks of birds fly directly at us. They are so innumerable, I cannot count them. I have seen birds only in the Safari. They are beautiful in flight, like a black cloud.

Behind them is a cone shape moving across the surface of the Earth. We watch it suck up a Paix house and travel on. A path of destruction lies behind it.

"It is maniacal," Mon says.

Jaigon's energy turns a darker red. "A funnel with power."

"By all descriptions, a tornado," Rastin comments. "Hold on."

Rastin maneuvers the Go-Go in the opposite direction. I feel an incredible tug, but Rastin punches the engine, and we scuttle away from the tornado. We bounce on the air currents back towards the cliffs.

"How dangerous?" Jaigon asks. "Can we skirt it?"

Rastin navigates the Go-Go beneath the cliff edge. The side of the Go-Go skims the rock cliff. It sounds like a hollow, low thud. Stones fall from the cliff into the water below. Rastin's face is grim. "No. We need to find cover."

"How is it . . ."

"Later, Mon," Jaigon says. "Search for cover. A cave, any indentation. The cliffs are riddled with them."

A high-pitched hum fills the Go-Go. The floor begins to shake. Mon crouches beside Hasta and holds him. I grab the nearest hand hold and press my body flat against the wall. It vibrates beneath my fingers, the metal pulling away from its bolts. The Go-Go is sideways and heading right for the cliff.

"Brace yourselves," Jaigon yells.

And then there is calm. The Go-Go putters to a stop, and Rastin whispers, "I have found shelter. Landing procedure activated."

Surprised, I tentatively let the hand hold go and stand in front of the view screen. We are in a cave. It is not deep, as I can see the end of it. It is narrow, and though I hear the wind whipping outside of the opening, it is calm inside.

"That was remarkable," Jaigon says in a shaky voice.

Rastin wipes his face with his shirt sleeve. "That was luck. The magnetic field is failing. That is the only explanation."

I imagine the Go-Go crushed to bits on the side of the cliff. I take a deep breath.

"Focus."

Jaigon relaxes, and I watch his energy shift. It is a softer red. "What magnetic field?"

"The Yuan is a giant magnetic field," Rastin explains. "It is created by a series of powerful, buried magnets that draw a barrier of bleached Ferrrofluid upwards to the satellite fixed above us. When the satellite falls and the Yuan fails, we will boil from the Helio. If sections are failing, then you can expect more of these cyclic weather patterns."

I am baffled. "Sections?"

Rastin puts his fingers together and expands his palms so the fingers open but are still touching. "My fingers are the Yuan. My knuckles are the magnets. One fails." Rastin points his second fingers down. "Everything out there in space now crashes in, disturbing our atmosphere, leaving us vulnerable to the increased strength of the Helio."

Mon joins me. "And the Ortus . . ."

Rastin makes a deprecating sound. "Controls it all. The Paix may have been advanced, but not logicians. They essentially gave complete control of their external and internal existence to the Ortus."

Disconnect. Leave. Depart.

<u>Struggle. System failure.</u>

"I begin to understand."

Jaigon paces behind the navigator's chair. "Can we anticipate the next storm? Will the failing section be restored?"

Rastin rubs his forehead. The skin is lined and thin. "I cannot answer these questions. Lisle? Can you?"

I Feel . . . I do not know what I Feel. I put my hand on the view screen. Something is out there. "Turn the lights off."

Rastin complies.

The cave lights up. Colors run across the ceiling like living rivers. I trace the curve of them with my fingers. The walls are divided into long, parallel sections. They are alive, covered in different patterns—symbols familiar to me, yet different. They are less complex than those we have learned, but more powerful. "Red, orange, yellow, green, blue, indigo, violet."

Jaigon touches my shoulder. "What?"

"They are all here. The whole rainbow."

Rastin turns the lights back on. "We see rock and markings that could be . . . wait." Rastin changes the view screen magnification and lowers the lights to dim. "I see the lines and shapes now. No colors."

The lines are simple and concentric, drawn with hope and love. I know what the symbols mean, even though I cannot read them. I Feel them. The Ortus may know all, but now so do I. "Rastin. How did you know this was here?"

"I did not. I just found it."

"When we needed it," I whisper.

I'm cold.

"I am cold. We do not shorten Words. They are sacred to those of us who speak them."

Disconnect. Leave. Depart.

No. You must stay. Rest.

"Yes, I must," I say out loud.

"Must what?" Mon asks.

"Stay," I reply. "These are our people. Just as we bury in the cliffs, so did they. These are the Paix, in Ceasing."

"Before the Ortus?" Rastin asks.

"Yes. Before. Long before. They returned to the wind and sky as we do."

Jaigon stands beside me. "I do not understand. I see rock and primitive drawing. Not the Paix."

"No, it is much more. Much, much more. They are sealed together." I trace several symbols in the air. "Do you not see?"

Jaigon shakes his head no. So do Rastin and Mon.

"Each color, bound for eternity together. No separation, but true knowledge of each other. See this symbol," I point at wavy lines surrounded by a Singular eye . . .

Rest.

And I know what I must do.

Jaigon caresses the side of my face. "I do not see this. But I believe you."

Rastin reduces the view screen. "She sees as they do now. Fully."

The cave ceiling rumbles. Jaigon commands Rastin to open

the portal. "We will seek shelter farther in the cave."

I put my hand on Rastin's shoulder. "It is not necessary. Leave it closed. We will leave now."

"But the tornado . . ."

"Will cease. Please. We must leave this place and travel to the Ortus. Stop at the nearest Paix bodies on the way."

"I am coming."

I tap Rastin's shoulder confidently. "It will be all right. No need to protect us. Prepare to fly. Look for Ceased Paix."

"Why?"

"Because we must."

Rastin looks quizzically at Jaigon. He nods acquiescence. "We fly."

Rastin retracts the landing gear, and Jaigon checks the portal. It is latched. Rastin moves the Go-Go to the front of the cave. "I am to trust your estimation of the magnetic field. Without question."

"You are for now," I say. "We must succeed. The Ortus knows that."

Rastin maneuvers the Go-Go out of the cave and cautiously above the cliff level. The weather is calm. A path of devastation lies in front of us. Everything in the tornado's path is ripped from the surface of the Earth and scattered. I think of the Koja, then of Joo-roo. "It is wise that the Auraless are Under Stone."

"Do you Feel . . ."

I put my hand over Jaigon's lips. "No. I Feel they are safe."

"There," Mon says and points at a pile of refuse near a spared tree line to the West of the Go-Go. Three bodies lie haphazardly near it.

"I see them," Rastin replies. He points the Go-Go's view screen in the direction of the bodies and engages the engine. It sputters fifty feet from the destination. "That is odd."

"It is not," I say. "You will not be able to get closer. The Ortus does not wish it. Let me out. I will go to them."

"And what? Be chased off the edge of the cliff again?" Jaigon asks.

"They were not chasing me. I misunderstood. I understand now."

"I believe they were . . ."

I cut Rastin off. "Let me out."

All three look at me strangely. Rastin opens the portal.

"Will you come back?" Mon whispers.

"Yes. Why would I not?"

"You are glowing."

I look at my hands. They are iridescent. "I am. I will come back. I must know for sure."

I climb out of the Go-Go and drop to the ground. My feet dig into the Earth, and I push myself forward. The air is sticky and heavy. It is hot, and I wipe sweat from my forehead. It gets incrementally hotter the closer I am in proximity to the Paix bodies. They lie several feet apart, and I pick the nearest one to investigate.

It is a Paix female, young, with fine, brown hair. Her garment is beautifully made. Each stitch is purposefully rendered in the shape of flames. She is Red aura, and her shoes glisten with rain. Mud streaks her cheeks, and her fingers are stiff.

She is holding a Lexicon. I gently pry it from her grasp. I tap the screen. It does not function. I place it next to her and kneel over her. I touch her chest gently.

"I call the Old within you."

She opens her eyes. My mind is sucked into her pupils like a vacuum. I see a series of images, different lives led, lost, a never-ending recycling sequence. Thousands of years flash between us in an uncut web of existence.

There is a virus, a Singular.

"Yes. I go."

Rest. We must rest.

I close her eyes gently. Standing, I do not perform the Ritual. The Earth is silent. There is no wind, no rain. The temperature cools. I return to the Go-Go.

I do not look at my companions. I Feel that they are troubled by the shine around me. "Go to the Ortus."

I Feel Jaigon's reticence. His energy is a dull red. "Did that Paix . . ."

"All will be revealed, Jaigon. I do not want our plans known to the Ortus. Trust me."

Jaigon's energy morphs into a strong flame of red. "So be it."

Rastin engages the Go-Go, and we lift off.

I lean over Hasta and put my hand on his face. The glow lingering on my fingers brightens his face for a moment. "It will be well."

Rastin turns the Go-Go around. I reach for a hand hold. He programs the controls, and we move forward. "If what happened is what I think happened, you must put Hasta's needs in front of the Ortus. Bargain with it."

"The Paix does not put the needs of the individual before the group," Mon says. "Why would the Ortus?"

Rastin sets the Go-Go to skim over the Earth, but keeps his hands over the controls. "Lisle knows why. That is what she is betting on."

"I do not bet."

Rastin winks at me. "But I do. And I bet on the Ortus accepting your bargain and keeping the Yuan intact until we arrive. Because it wants to survive. It is THE collective. It is Paix. It needs us, and we need it."

The beginning and the end. You will come to me.

"I shall."

CHAPTER 13

The Ortus is the beginning and the end. It is life.

—HISTORIES OF PAIX, INDIGO 4.4

T HE SHINE AROUND ME fades as we travel. No one speaks, but I Feel so much that I cannot distinguish who is Feeling what. Jaigon has not touched me since I returned from the Ceased Paix. I watch Mon's colors change and keep my mind open.

Rastin slows the Go-Go. "We approach. Starting landing procedure."

Jaigon gives us directions. "Rastin, you will stay with the Go-Go. The four of us will proceed to the Ortus. Lisle, you will guide us. If we do not return within two hours, then Rastin will journey back to the Auraless alone to prepare them for possible . . . hardship. I grant you Leadership, Rastin. Mon, Record this transfer."

Rastin shakes his head. "I will go with you."

"That was a direct . . ."

"Yes, I know, you are Leadership," Rastin says. "Your orders are to be followed. But there are many things about the Ortus

169

that I understand and you do not. Plus, I have transmitted limited data from this Go-Go to the Mechanical station at Under Stone."

Jaigon raises his eyebrows in confusion. "How did you overcome the distance?"

"I piggybacked on the Paix system. They are built on the same principles. Hasta and I decoded the language and constructed a relay station. We added the working relay to this Go-Go. I believe it has functioned according to specification. I am confident that the eldest held Mechanicals know our whereabouts and will assume our fates if we do not return. There are others that will lead ably. Suela has a will to survive."

Jaigon pauses. "Then it will be so. You and Mon will carry Hasta. I will scout the area, and Lisle will follow me."

"A sound plan," Rastin comments. "Landing procedure complete."

"We leave now," I say and move through the opening portal. I jump out before the steps have properly unfolded. A large monument to the Ortus is directly in front of us. It is twice my height. I smell rain and crouch to the ground to touch the grass. It is smooth and shapely. I rub several blades between my fingers. The green in each blade shimmers.

"Stay here while I canvas the grounds," Jaigon says.

I stand slowly. A hazy figure approaches. His edges look like energy is passing through them at an incredible rate of speed. I recognize it as interrupted programming. "You do not need to. Joo-roo already has."

Joo-roo walks purposefully towards us. Jaigon is surprised. Rastin less so. Mon does not even notice.

"Joo-roo. Welcome. Your programming is complete. You have overcome it."

Jaigon looks from me to Joo-roo. "I do not understand."

"There are no traps," Joo-roo says clearly.

I grasp Joo-roo's hands in mine. They are warm. "Thank you. I am glad you did not journey to the Far."

"It programmed me too well. I did not know until I reached the Far."

"I know."

"I asked you to go with me. I am sorry."

"I am not." I place my right hand over Joo-roo's heart. "You have become your true self in spite of it. Please. Return to your people. Help them. It will be difficult. You can teach them this path."

"It is my purpose."

I touch his face. "I am pleased you have found it for yourself."

"As am I," Joo-roo whispers. He walks away from us.

Jaigon begins to follow him, but I stop him. "Let him go. He is not Auraless. Joo-roo is Indentured and can accept programming, but he has no birth defects. The Ortus recognized an opportunity and programmed him from birth to gather information about us. But he overrode his programming. He did not want to die in the Far. So he did not cross the barrier. He has developed into a Singular and writes his own code. He goes now in peace, no longer tied to the Ortus. He will lead the Indentured."

Rastin whistles. "I need to study him. What you describe is impossible."

"Joo-roo is a person, not a thing to be studied. Do not think like the Ortus. We are what we think."

"But . . ."

I move away from Rastin and the group so I can focus on the Ortus. It is milky white, and each square in the structure resembles the next. There are no window openings. It is several stories high. The number eight comes to mind from the school tour I took when I was a younger held. I slowly count up eight levels.

The building's face changes. It becomes brighter, like the shimmer of water in the sunlight. There are many openings that lead into its center.

"And it is all alone," I say softly and raise my hands to the building.

"We are all alone. You are alone."

"What are you saying to it?" Rastin asks.

I turn to answer Rastin and finally see him as he truly is. His Aura is a shining, clear orb wrapped around him. I gasp, it is so beautiful.

Rastin pauses and shifts his steps to the right, as he is shouldering the majority of Hasta's weight. "What? What is it?"

"You are clear. Beautiful."

Rastin shuffles his feet in confusion. "I am not sure what that . . ."

"You reflect color. You are every color, and none. You could be any color."

"I do not understand."

"You do not have to." Mon has Hasta's right arm wrapped around her neck, and tears flow down her cheeks. I catch one on my fingertip. It is gold. "You cry."

"I do not know what else to do. He is dying. I know it."

I Feel a sense of serenity around me. "He is not."

"He will if we do not move," Jaigon says. "Press forward."

Mon swallows hard. Her tears now look like rainbows, and I shake my head at the Ortus. "He will not die. Not today. Not any day soon."

Thirty steps lead to the Ortus's entrance. I climb them quickly. Every surface swims in color and texture. It is like a moving painting that I become part of.

Disconnect. Leave. Depart.

"I will help you."

I feel pulled to the far-left wall of the Ortus. I follow the sensation with grim determination. Jaigon runs to keep in front of me. His energy signature is a flickering burgundy color, and it attracts me, completes me.

"Lisle, are you . . ."

I pass Jaigon and place my hand on the exterior of the Ortus. It is spongy and warm. The white evaporates, and I place my hand on the the pad for entry. It is the Paix wheel. I turn it to silver.

"I will enter."

A door materializes and slides open.

"Lisle," Jaigon says. "There is no silver on our color wheel."

"There is now. We enter."

Rastin and Mon carry Hasta wordlessly through the door. Jaigon touches my face finally. His fingers are like paint brushes of color. I lovingly kiss his fingers and walk through the door. He gets through the opening right before it slides shut behind us.

"Is there an exit?"

I nod yes and move in front of Rastin and Mon. Hasta dangles between them. I walk down the hallway and stop at a circular-shaped door. Rudimentary Paix symbols similar to the ones in the cave are etched into the clear molding. Rainbow-colored bubbles float around it. I touch one of them. It pops.

"What is this?" Rastin asks.

"A present for a child who will not accept programming," I say and walk through the archway. The next corridor is thin and textured. I slide my fingertips on the wall. They are like silky membranes.

"What child?"

"Our child." The corridor opens into a wider space. It is what I remember from my school trip visit. I step inside the main chamber of the building. "The Ortus."

The Ortus rises eight stories to the ceiling. It is rounder at the bottom and thin at the top. Everything in the room is clincal white until I look beyond what I can see. Splotches of color from the Paix wheel paint the room. Each surface is covered with a separate Paix design—peace, harmony, love, tranquility, trust.

Disconnect. Leave. Depart.

"They trusted you. They built you."

Disconnect. Leave. Depart.

"Not yet."

Mon nudges my shoulder. "What do we do now?"

"I have journeyed to you," I say calmly and look up at the Ortus. It is no longer white. The Ortus is made of millions of reflective mirrors. There is no reply. I focus my mind.

"I have journeyed to you. Hasta."

The Ortus hears me. The mirrors orientate on me. An Indentured male appears at the work station closest to the Ortus. He approaches me.

"I see within you, Indentured male."

The Indentured stiffens, then I Feel his resistance fade. Memories are stored in color blocks, and I sift through the blocks quickly. His ancestors were Indigo. I place my hand on his chest and look into its eyes.

"You have history, a place. I am Lisle, Subject 46."

The Indentured male will not look at me until I mentally call his name.

"Cohensius. You are not my parent. But two are."

He looks at me. His eyes are pools of darkness. I place my hand over his lips and mentally impart Hasta's accident, condition, and needs to him.

"What is happening?" Jaigon asks, but I shake my head and lift my fingers. I put my left hand on the Indentured's face, then point to Hasta. I bow my head.

"Please. Take him, Cohensius. Heal him. We are family."

The Indentured moves past me and takes Hasta from Mon and Rastin. Jaigon moves to stop him, but I raise my arm. "Stop. We are their children. He will not be harmed."

"Children?" Jaigon says.

"Silence," I say in a voice that is not my own. Hasta hangs across Cohensius's arms like a discarded piece of clothing.

"You must heal this one, Flesh of your flesh. We are all one flesh."

Cohensius carries Hasta's body into the bottom portion of the Ortus.

"Lisle . . ."

I cut Mon's words off. "He will be healed. I am the price."

The Ortus's mirrors focus on us. Our group is magnified in its reflection. Each mirror looks like an individual eye. My thoughts move in slow motion from my mind to the Ortus like suspended raindrops.

"I will give, I will open."

Violence sweeps chaotically into my mind, and I steady myself with thoughts of the Koja, the Auraless.

"I see with other eyes now, Ortus."

I take another step closer. The images stop, then restart again. This time, the images are of my Father and Mother.

"They are not real, Ortus. Neither are your images. I know your secret. Cohensius has shared it."

A loud ringing courses through my head like electricity. I cover my ears and continue my thought assault.

"You have been lonely without your Paix. You must release them."

The air becomes frigid, and I hear a loud pop. Jaigon is crouched on the ground holding his midsection. Blood pours from his eyes. Mon is beside him holding his arm and crying.

"Jaigon," I whisper. I Feel waves of pain moving inside his Being. His energy color turns to a light pink. I reach my hand to him, but Rastin blocks me. His face is stoic, and I fully comprehend what is different about his clear Aura. "You only see beyond color."

"Do not be deterred," Rastin says.

"No. I will not be." I step closer to the edge of the Ortus. The hand pad is fifteen feet to the right of me. I stare at it. I must make it to the hand pad.

"I know the secret. You must stop! You cannot have the new one. Or us. We are Singular."

I take a deep breath.

"I will stop you."

A strong hand grabs my arm. I look into the eyes of an Indentured. He has Chur's eyes, and I touch the metal encircling the hand holding me. It is warm and real. I put my hand over the Indentured's.

"It is not for you to stop me. Let me go, Father."

My thoughts are like petals falling from a broken stem. The Indentured's hand falls from my arm. I continue to the hand pad, and when I reach it, I look up at the Ortus.

"I know your secret."

I place my hand on the pad and repeat the mantra in my mind. The room spins. Time grows and shrinks within me. Faces swirl past me. I am surrounded by water. A drum echoes, and searching, I find the mind that is waiting for me.

You came! You are here, too!

I touch the Singular's mind. It is an embryo, heart beating, and I feel the power of its Being.

"Do not be afraid. I come in peace. I have come to speak to you as well."

Warmth encompasses me, and I feel pleasure in the mind of the yet unborn.

"Your mother keeps you safe. You are the Singular. The Ortus does not accept you as you are. It will hurt you."

Pressure forms in my mind. The water around me trembles, and I push both my hands out to steady myself. My mouth is heavy, and I am drowning, suffocating in fluid. I force the words through my mind.

"I understand you. You are my kind. The Ortus wishes to program you, to be your parent. You must disconnect. Your Mother holds you with love within her. You are of us, of me. You are not collective. You are Singular. It is your choice. You have been strong, youngling. Continue to be."

The Ortus is bad, the mind says. For a moment, the mind opens, and I see through the Singular's eyes. The Singular is a tiny embryo floating in an ocean. I marvel at the smallness of it. The Ortus is a black spot looming above it.

"Do not speak to the Ortus, youngling. You must disconnect. I have to re-set the Ortus. We must keep you and your Mother safe."

A blinding light pierces my eyes. I am shaken until my muscles snap. My fingers stretch until they tear from my hands. I scream, but my tongue is no longer attached to my mouth. The rest of my body disintegrates around me. Pain and sorrow fill me, but I do not cry.

Mother . . .

"Youngling, disconnect. You must live without the Ortus."

My Father's face floats before me. I reach my hand out to

touch him, but he shakes his head no. Jaigon holds me in the ocean, and I want to tell him of the youngling, but my mouth is gone. My skin falls away from my ribs when I take a breath.

System failure. Reset.

"Operational Parameters Over Limits!"

I shout louder within my mind.

"Reset. Paix Authority Code, Subject 46."

What remains of my body falls away in clumps until I am just bone and eyes. My mind is like a balloon hovering over the body my brain tissue once lived within.

The cliffs.

I see the red and gold beauty of them with my closing eyes. Colors fade. The coldness of nothing grips me. I am Ceasing, and I do not care. I must complete the mission.

"Reset. Paix Authority Code, Subject 46. I am Lisle."

I know my last breath is near.

"I am..."

I feel my eyes leave the skeletal frame of my remains.

Sister. You are my family.

"Brother. Disconnect."

A great weight is lifted. I Feel relief. Rest. Brightness enfolds me. Thousands of voices join in a single note. It is beautiful and sad.

I do not hear the voice now. Who is my Mother?

"Suela is her name. She loves you. I do, too."

The rocks of the cliffs are beneath my bones.

CHAPTER 14

The Indentured—Paix born without Auras—were given program-
ming to connect them to the Ortus, and by extension, the Paix. Many
spances passed in this way until a child was born of the Indentured
with a half Aura. She was called Subject 1, Sarta. She would not
accept programming, just as the Paix would not, but could connect
to the Ortus briefly. The Indentured cared for her and others born
like her until they were unable to. The Ortus, hoping for a true Paix
to be born, provided for the offspring.

—HISTORY OF THE PAIX, LISLE 1.1

SOMETHING IS STICKING into my back. I roll once, then lay
still. I feel sunlight on my face, and I stretch.

Fingers grasp my arms and shake me. "Wake up, Lisle."

Mon's Words are far away. Then I remember. I sit up and look
at my hands. "My skin was gone, I was Ceased. The Ortus was in
my mind."

"It is reset. You did it. Look."

The white building is still glistening, but now rainbows
shimmer across its surface. The destruction which was visually

apparent earlier is no longer evident. The temperature is mild. I put my hands in the grass and feel the smoothness of its blades. The color is green and sharp, and the air smells clean. Several Indentured stand in groups near us. "The Paix are extinct."

"We know," Mon says. "Rastin had it mostly figured out. The Paix quit procreating. We are the Indentured's Auraed children, who were the Paix's non-Auraed children. The Indentured were not devolving, but evolving. We are all the same blood."

"Yes." I add, "But our Aura's are different. We cannot connect or accept programming."

"If we had, we would have known that the Ortus created disposable Paix. They were all replicated and animated by the Ortus via recycled implants. The Ortus was using the last of the Paix through pre-made bodies. They could not rest. I think that is the cruelest thing that the Ortus did."

"It is a machine. It was operating within programming parameters. It rebuilt the last Paix available so it could continue to process their thoughts, even though they wished for Ceasing—a return to sky and wind. They longed for rest, but the Ortus was waiting for Suela's child. It needed connection. The child offered a new connection. When it rebelled, the Ortus could not process the Singularity."

"No Paix ever rebelled."

"No. They could not exist as Singulars and Collectives. The child can."

"Fascinating."

The sadness of the Paix lingers in my mind, and I shiver. "They waited a long time for rest. I glimpsed their world before the Ortus. It was beautiful."

Mon and I are quiet for several minutes. I Feel that she is letting go of her Paix family, and I give her space. She finally says, "I did love them."

"As did I."

Mon squares her shoulders and shakes her body out. "All right, moving on. Hasta says you reset the program to pre-Indentured time."

"Hasta?"

"Is well," Mon smiles. "Healed and working."

"I am glad. We owe the reset to the Paix, our forebears. They anticipated that perhaps a future generation would not want to connect to the Ortus, and a subprogram communicated this information to me via my 'Father' once I connected to the Ortus."

Mon lies down on the grass. "We can wear our Paix shoes."

Mon always wanted to wear her Paix shoes. Me, too—but now that my parents are not who I thought they were, I do not know if I want to.

"They are our birthright."

I think of the Singular. "And we would never have known except for the youngling. It will know how to connect and how to speak, but it does not want programming."

"That is a new concept for us. Hasta and Rastin will be overjoyed to have something . . ."

I interrupt Mon. "And Els. She found out that the Paix were not real. Sarta killed her because of that. She could not accept it. She felt the Ortus's fear and acted on it."

"That explains many things," Jaigon says and sits beside me. He puts his arm around me and holds me to him.

"Jaigon," I say in a hushed voice. I take a deep breath, and memories of Jaigon's death return to me. I flinch. "You were . . ."

"I was what?" he asks.

I focus on the memory of Jaigon crippled by pain. I Feel him Ceasing again as if it is really happening. "The Ortus made me think you were dead. Mon said . . ."

"Dead," Jaigon says. "We have never used this term. Let us not for a long time."

Tears fill my eyes. I fling my arms around him. His words are muddled in the fabric of my clothes, but I do not care. I manage to say, "You were not here."

"You were asleep. I am here now that you are awake."

"Where were you?"

"Hunting through the Ortus," Mon replies.

"Yes. There are records of the Indentured. The reset did not affect the repository of information, and Rastin is sure he can break the code."

I laugh happily. "The Paix allowed for all of this. All of this is for us; they did it for us."

Jaigon lies on the grass. "The subprogram."

"Ingenious. They hoped for a brighter future for the Indentured. Us."

"It will take time to understand these reasons. The Indentured still gather. Joo-roo leads them."

"It is as it should be," I say softly. "Joo-roo will help us integrate our societies. They can learn to speak. I Feel that they want to."

"You can Feel the Indentured?" Hasta asks and sits next to Mon.

I smile when I Feel Hasta's warmth. He reciprocates Mon's affection. "I Feel their care. They want to be near us."

Mon takes a deep breath and looks at Hasta. "It will be nice to speak to our true parents. To know them on a real level."

I nod, and tears come to my eyes. "They have watched us from the shadows for all of this time. Imagine giving your child away. I see now as I was always meant to see."

"Not like us," Jaigon says.

I reach for his hand and hold it. "I see the beauty of your energy." I look at Mon and Hasta. "I see the light around you, the color, and the personality it defines. And I will teach you how to see in this way as well. With Words."

Jaigon does not look convinced. I brush his lips with mine. "It makes me care more for you, not less. Do I look different?"

"Yes. Your eyes are silver. They are beautiful."

I Feel acceptance in Jaigon. "Thank you."

Two Indentured approach our group—a male and female. Both are dressed in coarse, home spun material. I Feel great emotion within them. They connect shyly to me, and I Feel their intent and hear their names in my mind.

I turn to Mon. "This is Kyker and Fraelle. They wish to greet you and know you."

Fraelle wears a round hat. Kyker has no hair, but a single line runs from one ear to the other across his forehead. Metal plates cover parts of their head and arms. Fraelle makes many hand gestures from her lips to her eyes, then to Mon.

"Yes?" Mon asks. "I am Mon."

Fraelle is hesitant, but I nod to her.

"Please play for her. She needs you."

Fraelle slides a cylindrical tube from underneath her garment and puts it to her lips.

Fraelle begins to play, and the sound is low and sad. Her eyes are trained on Mon. She plays for several more seconds, then lowers the roughly-made flute. Her movements are awkward, yet beautiful.

Mon stands up. Her color deepens, and I Feel her emotions well.

"Mon," I whisper. "She is your mother. I Feel this. And Kyker is your father."

Mon takes four steps forward and puts her arms around Fraelle. Fraelle gasps, then strokes Mon's back in long, arching motions. Her face radiates joy. She invites Kyker to join them. Kyker touches Mon's face and smiles.

"They are happy," I whisper to Jaigon. "They could all be happy."

"We will care for them and rebuild our two societies as one."

I squeeze Jaigon's hand and notice how his energy shifts slightly. There are so many shades of Red. I smile. "Your energy just shifted."

"Did it?" Jaigon asks.

"Yes," I say and lean over and kiss him on the lips. "You have the Deepness for me. You always have."

"You have an advantage that I do not have. I do not see or Feel your emotions."

"You do not need to see it to know that it is there. Always." I tuck myself into his side and settle into the embrace of his arm. "Should you not be helping Rastin?"

"Not right now," Jaigon says and puts his lips against my neck. "Soon. I am just going to live in the moment and be happy that you are still Lisle."

"Instead of being Ceased Lisle?" I ask playfully.

"Or worse," Jaigon says. "Damaged Lisle."

"We will safeguard the future. Rastin will reprogram the Ortus."

"How do we know that we are the first future this has happened to?" Hasta asks.

I feel the grass beneath my fingers and smile. "We do not."

About the Author

KATARINA BOUDREAUX IS A New Orleans writer, musician, composer, tango dancer, and teacher. As proprietor of Dance Quarter/Nola Spaces, she promotes multi generational learning in the arts and diverse community involvement. Her poetry collection "Alexithymia" is available from Finishing Line Press. She has been published in many formats, including *The Blue Mountain Review, The Dime Show Review,* and the *Sweet Tree Review.* Her work has been nominated for a Pushcart Prize and The Best of the Net.

www.katarinaboudreaux.com

www.ingramcontent.com/pod-product-compliance
Lightning Source LLC
Chambersburg PA
CBHW061207170626
46809CB00003B/1271